Run

James A. Moore

Run

James A. Moore

AN IMPRINT OF PENGUIN GROUP (USA) Inc.

Run

RAZORBILL

Published by the Penguin Group
Penguin Young Readers Group
345 Hudson Street, New York, New York 10014, U.S.A.
Penguin Group (USA) Inc., 375 Hudson Street, New York, New York 10014, U.S.A.
Penguin Group (Canada), 90 Eglinton Avenue East, Suite 700, Toronto, Ontario, Canada M4P 2Y3 (a division of Pearson Penguin Canada Inc.)
Penguin Books Ltd, 80 Strand, London WC2R 0RL, England
Penguin Ireland, 25 St Stephen's Green, Dublin 2, Ireland (a division of Penguin Books Ltd)
Penguin Group (Australia), 250 Camberwell Road, Camberwell, Victoria 3124, Australia (a division of Pearson Australia Group Pty Ltd)
Penguin Books India Pvt Ltd, 11 Community Centre, Panchsheel Park, New Delhi–110 017, India
Penguin Group (NZ), 67 Apollo Drive, Mairangi Bay, Auckland 1311, New Zealand (a division of Pearson New Zealand Ltd)
Penguin Books (South Africa) (Pty) Ltd, 24 Sturdee Avenue, Rosebank, Johannesburg 2196, South Africa

Penguin Books Ltd, Registered Offices: 80 Strand, London WC2R 0RL, England

10 9 8 7 6 5 4 3 2 1

ISBN 978-1-59514-305-1

Library of Congress Cataloging-in-Publication Data is available

Printed in the United States of America

Chapter One

Cody Laurel

HE COULDN'T TELL HOW long they'd been driving. It felt like a few hundred hours. Any way you looked at it, Cody was glad when they finally stopped. Despite the protests of cramped legs, he sprinted for the public restrooms. He was so full of piss his teeth were damned near floating, and he was going to explode if he waited too much longer.

The truck stop was a compromise. Hunter Harrison wanted to keep moving. In particular he wanted to get to Chicago and the address he had tucked in his jeans before anyone could warn the people they were after that they were coming. Cody sort of wanted that too, but what he really wanted was a place to sleep. It felt like forever since any of them had gotten any rest. Instead of living his normal life, Cody had run away from home, met up with the strangers he was now traveling with and discovered that he had a monster hiding away inside of his body. Then, just to keep things from getting boring, he'd decided that continuing on the run with the rest of the kids in the same situation was a better idea than going home and facing his parents' wrath. Not exactly the cozy nap he wanted to have. Now he was settling for a meal and more driving rather than much-needed sleep.

Instead of riding straight through the night or stopping at a hotel, they entered the Truckadero Truck Stop, which promised good eats and twenty showers. He wanted to eat and stretch his legs. Kyrie and Tina were both desperate for showers, and Gene wanted to sulk some more. He was doing a great job of pouting. Hunter wanted to drive. He kept looking over his shoulder like any second someone was going to come along and wreck everything.

Hunter. He was the one who had it the worst, maybe. He had to deal with Joe Bronx.

Just a few days ago, Cody'd had a real life, a normal life, like the rest of the people he was riding with—the ones Joe Bronx condescendingly called the Failures. A normal life. A dad, a mom and friends. Okay, the friends were geeky, but they still counted. He'd been daydreaming about adventures for as long as he could remember and now? Well, now he was having a hell of a time trying to figure out exactly what was happening. And while there was definitely some action and adventure going on, he wasn't having a great time.

There was him and there were four other kids the same age, who were, maybe, just as screwed up as he was.

And then there were the others. The Others, the Hydes to their Jekylls.

Cody flushed and zipped and walked over toward the sinks. Somebody with a warped sense of humor had drawn a face on the mirror, and as Cody approached, his reflected face slid into the center of the crude picture. The result was a distortion of his features. His reflection looked almost like it had been swallowed by a bigger face. Normally he'd have thought it was a stupid picture, would have maybe even gotten a little chuckle out of the image—okay, very little, but still. Now? Now the image was unsettlingly close to what his life had become.

The Others. He didn't know much about them. Whenever they showed up, he went away, swallowed by the other personality hiding inside of him. Hank. The other self inside of him chose the name Hank, and Cody doubted it was a coincidence. Hank Chadbourne was one of the class bullies back home. He'd kicked the crap out of Cody at least a dozen times. He was directly responsible for at least half the panic attacks that had left Cody a little on the neurotic side over the years. Hank Chadbourne was a monster, pure and simple. But he was a human monster.

And somewhere inside of Cody was another mind, but more than that there was another body, physically stronger, faster and tougher than Cody could hope to be. And when the time was right that other personality, Hank, liked to come out and play.

Yeah. He was a load worse than Hank Chadbourne could ever be. Cody closed his eyes and felt his heart beat faster. Hank was inside of him, watching. He could feel him. Maybe it was that way for all of them, or maybe it wasn't. He didn't know for sure. If he focused hard on it, he could remember little bits and pieces of the things Hank had done. Hank was fearless. Cody was . . . not. Cody thought about maybe asking Amanda Summers out to a movie or something, someday. Nothing too big or too fancy, because she'd probably run screaming. Amanda was hot, killer legs, nice butt and one of the biggest racks at school. She was also one of the rare girls who would actually smile when she caught him looking her over. So, yeah, he figured he could ask her out someday. You know, after hell froze over. Until then there was too much of a chance that she'd laugh in his face or maybe sic Hank and Glenn Wagner on him to beat him to death. There were a million ways that actually talking to Amanda could result in humiliation or failure.

He could close his eyes and still feel Hank's lips kissing a complete stranger, could feel Hank's hands pulling the girl in closer as the kiss got steamier. He opened his eyes fast at that, because the last thing he needed was a stiffy to advertise to the girls he was traveling with. His reflection looked back at him and blushed.

"Yeah. Tina'd chew you up and spit out the bones,

dude." He spoke solely to hear someone speak. He'd just finished talking to himself when Gene Rothstein came into the restroom with a wrinkled nose and a look on his face that said he'd maybe just swallowed a bug and it was still squirming.

Gene was another Failure. Gene was nice enough—average looking, if a bit tall—definitely in better shape than Cody. But that was hardly challenging since Cody had all the muscle tone of wet spaghetti. Dark hair and tanned complexion, Gene was the sort who was destined for middle management or just maybe a life as an accountant, if Cody had to guess. He liked Gene. Gene's other half, well, that was a different story. If he thought about the kid's counterpart, all he got was a mental image of a really, really pissed-off guy with longer, darker hair, a broad face and a serious need to cause pain to anything that got in his way. If he closed his eyes and thought about Gene, he could also tap into Hank's perspective of Gene. Hank was pretty sure he could beat Gene's counterpart into putty. Cody didn't want to test that theory. Hank could be as brave as he wanted, but Cody had a serious allergy to pain.

"Did something die in here?" Gene waved his hand around, like it would maybe get rid of the smell of urine and flatulence.

"Dude, it's like a locker room, only concentrated. Old pee and bad ventilation." Cody smiled. Despite the fact that

Gene was kind of prissy, he was mostly okay.

Gene looked at him and pointed down to the right. "Out the door and that way to the showers."

"Wasn't planning on taking one."

Gene looked him in the eye and shook his head. "You should. You smell like old gym socks."

Cody started to open his mouth and say something, but Gene wasn't done. "Listen. I'm doing you a favor. Neither of the girls we've been traveling with are the sort to say it, but we're all driving in a car. They're going to smell you and decide you disgust them. Clean up. It'll wake you up, and you need to stop smelling so bad. Seriously."

"Whatever." Cody felt himself blushing and stormed out of the room. Maybe he didn't like Gene so much after all. But despite his indignation, he headed for the showers.

Tina had given him some money. He used five dollars of it to purchase a shower, complete with travel-sized shampoo and soap. Gene was right about one thing. He didn't want to smell like an unwashed teenager around Kyrie or Tina. They were almost willing to talk to him. Best not to let a chance like that slip past.

While he showered, he closed his eyes.

And felt Hank inside of him, waiting, biding his time.

He took no comfort from that notion.

Hunter Harrison

Chapter Two

HUNTER ATE VORACIOUSLY. He was hungry. Even when he wasn't hungry, he wanted food. He blamed Joe for that. Months of living on canned crap was about enough to ruin his self-control when it came to real food, and much as he hadn't wanted to stop driving, he had to admit the food at the restaurant was better than he'd expected. He'd finished his steak and was busily wiping his plate clean with a chunk of dinner roll.

The next booth over was occupied by two men who sat leaning toward each other and murmuring softly. They spoke so as not to be heard, but he heard them anyway. He could just make out that they were upset about the cost of fuel for their trucks. From beyond the grizzled men he saw Tina Carlotti heading in his direction, her wet hair pulled back in a tight ponytail and her eyes locked on the table. She was petite: a tiny, olive-skinned, dark-haired girl who looked twelve at the most. But she was fifteen, same as he was. Probably had the same birth date, assuming that they were actually *born*. Hard to say. He didn't know all of the details of being created in a genetics lab. Regardless, she had a lot in common with him.

Kyrie Meriwether was shadowing the shorter girl. She was also fifteen, but aside from that and being a girl, she had almost nothing in common with Tina. She was several inches taller and had fairer skin with blonde hair, green eyes, and a body that caught the eyes of almost every guy and probably a few of the girls too. Kyrie was in a different league, and even when she was trying to dress down, she stood out. She was currently wearing a T-shirt that did nothing to hide her assets and jeans that Hunter found himself envying—they were, after all, very close to her form.

Both of the men at the booth stopped talking about the unfortunate cost of gasoline and started murmuring about what they would like do with the two girls heading in their direction. They weren't exactly loud, but they weren't whispering either. Hunter had no doubt that Tina and Kyrie could hear them.

Hunter repressed a sudden flash of anger that came with hearing them. Even if he wanted to throw down with the two guys, they were easily a hundred pounds bigger than he was and they looked like they'd had more than their share of fights over the years. Sure, they were flabby, but something had to be holding all that fat up, right?

As she closed in on the table, Tina and fired a look at them that would have frozen boiling water. "Okay, first, that's disgusting. Even if you weren't both old enough to be my daddy, I wouldn't even consider it. And neither would she. You're both too fat and we ain't that desperate. Go buy a hooker."

Hunter barely suppressed a wild burst of laughter. He should have known he wouldn't have to worry about protecting Tina. She was tough as nails.

The truckers looked less amused. Tina slid into the booth next to Hunter and never batted an eye as she reached for one of his fries. He resisted the urge to slap her hand away. He wasn't all that hungry anymore, and even if he thought she was being was rude, he wasn't about to piss her off.

Kyrie slid in across from them and smiled. She didn't say anything, but Hunter didn't much care. He could have stared at her for a week without getting bored.

Tina caught the waitress's eye and gestured her over. "Need some food here. I'm gonna starve to death, I swear it."

The truckers were still sitting at the next table. The one who was facing them looked at Tina and scowled. "You need something to plug that mouth." Hunter couldn't tell if he was flirting or just being a weenie. "Or you could just learn to keep it shut."

Tina bristled. "Yeah? You could maybe learn from your own example there, bubba. Keep that mouth of yours shut and you could lose a few hundred pounds and have a chance with the ladies."

Hunter swallowed and shook his head. "Don't, Tina."

"What?" She shot him a murderous look. "He started it. I don't need Porky Pig over there or his good buddy saying anything to me or about me."

Porky Pig slid out from the booth, heaving his substantial weight up and then yanking his jeans to where he wanted them. He was a big man, standing easily six feet tall, and Hunter was already imagining how badly the guy was going to beat him to death even before the trucker started heading in his direction.

"You need to teach your little girlfriend some manners, buddy." The guy was looking right at him. "Before her mouth gets you beat to hell."

Kyrie turned to look at the man coming their way, a worried expression on her pretty face. Tina was actually sliding her skinny body around until she was on her knees in the booth, and Hunter had a terrifying flash of insight. She had every intention of taking the guy on. His hand moved to grab the back of her pants at the belt level, and he shook his head. "No. Don't you do it, Tina."

"You got a problem with me, fat boy, you talk to me." She was doing it, she was actually provoking the guy. Then, to Hunter: "I don't need him fighting my fights."

The saddest part was, she sounded absolutely serious.

"You shut your trap, girly."

The waitress was heading for them, a worried look on her face. "Billy Ray, you need to calm down. Todd said he wasn't gonna have you fighting with anyone else now, you hear me?"

Billy Ray. Of course Porky's real name was Billy Ray. He looked like a Billy Ray.

"It's all good. Billy Ray was just going to sit down like a gentleman and behave himself." The rumbling voice came from behind the trucker before the man could say anything. Even if he'd wanted to get all chatty, the hand that clamped down on his shoulder and squeezed seemed to take most of the fight out of him. Hunter was looking right at him. He saw the wince of pain and the way the man's knees almost buckled when the hand squeezed.

Big hand. Really big. Half a second later, he saw Hank's face peering around from behind the trucker. Hank's grin was pure piss and vinegar. There was no kindness in his expression.

Hank. Cody's Other was out and in control. Hank was huge. He dwarfed the trucker, which meant he was exactly the right size to scare a black bear.

"Go ahead, Billy Ray. Sit down nice and calm and we'll all pretend everything's cool. I'm just here to have a nice meal with my little sister and her friends, and you're just here to sit down and jaw with your friend." Hank's voice was a low purr as he leaned over Billy Ray, letting the man see exactly how big he was.

Billy Ray looked at Hank, then looked at the waitress, then back at Tina, who was smiling toothily at him, then back again at Hank.

Finally he decided to sit down. Hank patted his back cheerily and slipped past him in the booth, sitting next to Kyrie, who looked even smaller in comparison to his hulking figure.

Hunter felt himself relax. He'd sort of expected Hank to break the man's back, or maybe just flat-out kill him. He hadn't actually, technically met this Other. Tina had. Gene had. Kyrie had. Joe Bronx had. But not Hunter. He'd been too busy being a monster himself when Hank showed up. He only recognized the brute as Cody's Other because of the pictures the Others had taken of themselves so that the Failures would know who they were dealing with.

The waitress who had witnessed the entire thing nodded and started taking orders while Hunter looked over Hank and the two truckers behind him. Hank didn't seem worried at all about turning his back on the two apes. Cody would have been sweating all over himself and maybe trying to find a way to squirm between Tina and Hunter on their side of the booth, but Hank was calm and cool and in control. Weird. He'd half expected someone with all the manners of the Tasmanian devil.

Hank looked him over, a small smile playing on his face. He only stopped staring to order his food. The clothes he was wearing were beginning to rip at the seams—which wasn't surprising, really, since they'd been on Cody only a few minutes earlier. Cody was like the runt of the litter, but Hank? Hank was a brute any way you looked at it.

When Hank was done ordering, he leaned forward on the table and planted his elbows. He didn't look at Hunter but directed his gaze toward Tina. "Anyone ever tell you to back up on the 'tude?"

Tina eyed him right back. "Like I'd listen."

Hank let out a bark of laughter and leaned back. Then his eyes flickered over to Hunter again, taking his measure. He didn't seem overly impressed with what he was seeing. On the other hand, at least he wasn't getting angry. That seemed like a big plus.

"Where are we?" Hank's question seemed casual. Maybe having Joe Bronx dictating his life had made Hunter paranoid, but he didn't trust the relaxed demeanor. There had to be another agenda, didn't there?

"Almost to Illinois," Hunter replied.

"Cool." Hank smiled and leaned forward again. The bruiser seemed to have too much energy to sit still. "So we can maybe say hello to Evelyn today? Or you think tomorrow?"

Evelyn Hope was the reason they were driving from Boston to Chicago. The woman in question was, if they were right in what they'd learned, the reason that they existed in the first place. They were the genetic experiments that had gone wrong in the efforts to make perfect spies, assassins, or soldiers. He wasn't really sure exactly which. They were the Failures. The ones that didn't quite work out. They were supposed to be dead and instead they were, well, they were here, and they shared the same problem. There were two people in each body. It wasn't working out very well. Evelyn Hope was just that, really: their last hope to fix the problem.

Hunter stared hard. It was difficult to deal with this. He'd never spoken to "Hank," but the guy had information that almost nobody had. He was in on what Joe and the other counterparts were up to, and it was unsettling. More importantly, the Other had already spent private time with Joe Bronx a couple of days before, shortly after Joe, Hunter's Other half, revealed to them that they were all connected. That was something most of them hadn't done. The thought made Hunter nervous. Joe was his Other, true, but they'd never met face-to-face and he knew that his Hyde had been planning things on his own for a long time.

And yet, the massive figure sitting across from him was also Cody, who was short and skinny and bordered on mousy. Thinking about it made his head ache.

Tina rolled her eyes and elbowed Hunter in the rib cage. "You go to sleep over there? It's rude not answering a question." She looked at Hank and answered for him before he could respond. "Hunter thinks we can get there today. We just need to eat and then we're on the way again."

Hank looked at her again, smile lines around his eyes. "You're cute when you're growling."

Tina did the absolutely unexpected and blushed. Last thing he would have ever thought the girl even capable of. Hunter thought she basically ate nails, and here she was getting shy around the looming figure of Cody's Other.

"I don't know what to say to that." Tina looked away, and Hank chuckled.

Gene came from the direction of the showers, which meant that all of them had finally gotten cleaned up and they could be on the road that much sooner. Gene was tall and lean and normally very reserved. All of this, of course, was really just first impressions—because they'd barely had a chance to get to know each other yet. Hunter got a good feeling off the kid, even if he thought Gene was a little on the fussy side. The guy looked at dirt like it was a personal insult to all he believed in. He doubted Gene had ever so much as made a mud pie.

Gene looked at Hank like he might be a sleeping pit bull; like there was a very strong chance the Other might suddenly leap at him.

Tina's hip smacked against Hunter's side. "Scoot. We gotta make room for Gene. No way he's fitting in next to

Godzilla over there."

Hank slowly smiled. "I always preferred King Kong."

Tina looked Hank over. "Yeah, well, King Kong had more hair than you."

Hunter shook his head even as he slid over. She really was fearless.

Gene sat next to Tina and crowded Hunter into the corner of the booth. Hunter felt his knee brush Kyrie's and had to suppress a blush of his own. Damn, she was gorgeous.

For her part Kyrie kept looking at Hank, half dwarfed by the size of him as he sat next to her on the other side of the booth.

Hank leaned back and draped his arm over the back of the seat. He seemed oblivious to the look that the trucker behind him cast his way. Maybe he didn't care. Maybe he didn't need to care.

There were too many maybes. Hunter didn't have the answers, not any more than the other people at the table did.

He observed while the whole group settled in and talked. Trying to think through the answers they'd gotten to the questions that had haunted him ever since he woke up five months earlier with amnesia.

He struggled with it. There were memories in his head that he could barely access, faces that should have meant something to him but had no connection to his world. He closed his eyes and saw a woman's face and thought she might be his mother, saw a man's and guessed that perhaps he was seeing his father; there was a boy in his memories—younger than him—perhaps a little brother or a cousin. Or all of them could have been faces from a magazine ad for all he knew. There were no connections, only the feeling that they were somehow important.

Around him the others at the table started eating, chowing down on the food that the waitress brought for them, mostly massive burgers and heaping piles of fries, but Kyrie ordered a tomato stuffed with tuna salad and already looked like she was regretting not getting the larger meal. Both Hank and Tina had also ordered large bowls of chili that looked like they were at least half grease. Hunter had already eaten, and his head ached from driving down the road and staring so hard. He knew how to drive but had no idea how he'd learned. Maybe it was something that Joe Bronx had mastered and he was just getting the benefits without the training. He wasn't sure how it worked. What he did know was that they were all going to be wearing baggy clothes from now on. He'd done some shopping while they were all showering, and before they left, he'd suggest they go back and change again. Instead of clothes like they'd all been traveling in, he'd picked up several sets of running pants and sweats. It was that or stretch the stuff they were wearing. Why Bronx had never made the switch was one of those things he'd never know. That was the one of the problems with their situation: they were still new to all of this, and they were learning as they went along.

According to what Joe Bronx had said, he and the others were supposed to be soldiers, sleepers who could be trained in military combat and tactics so that their bigger, far stronger selves could go into battle with the full knowledge of how to fight. Did that work both ways? Or had somebody actually shown him how to drive on his own? The amnesia thing was getting old. He had no way to know, not yet. Not without finding answers from Evelyn Hope or someone else connected to his past.

But maybe Evelyn Hope would have answers. He had to believe it. His hand moved to his hip, touching the sheet of paper in his back pocket. There was an address on that paper. The address was where Evelyn Hope was supposed to be waiting. All they had to do was find her, and if it went the way they wanted, she would be able to answer their questions, to give them back their lives somehow.

He understood that he would never be free of Joe Bronx, not if what his Other had said was true. But maybe he could find out about his family, about the life he used to have. And maybe, somehow, he could get back to that life again.

Evelyn Hope was his last chance, he supposed. He dug the envelope out of his pocket and looked at it again. There was a return address. He read it silently and then read it again aloud. "Josh Warburton."

"Who?" Tina looked up from the bowl of chili she was attacking.

"Josh Warburton. He's the one who wrote the letter to Evelyn Hope. He's in Chicago too. If they work together, maybe he can help us get answers."

Tina shrugged her response.

Gene nodded. "It's a possibility. He might work in the same offices now, or maybe he at least knows about Janus and can tell us where we can find information if Evelyn Hope proves useless."

"So how do we know they'll help us, anyway?" Kyrie's voice was small, but she looked directly at Hunter as she spoke.

Before he could answer, Hank spoke up. "We don't know. It's just all we have to work with right now." He angled his body toward Kyrie. "When you don't have anything to work with, you have to start sniffing for clues. Joe said this was all he had after years of looking, so we sort of have to try for this."

Hunter tuned out the conversation, trying to remember anything at all from his past that might help them. He shook his head. He couldn't go on this way. He had to escape from the endless transformations—and soon.

Evelyn Hope had to have the answers; that was all there was to it.

Around him the others were laughing at something Hank had said. Hunter hadn't been listening closely enough to hear what it was, but he was glad the others were having fun. They all needed a little more laughter in their lives.

Chapter Three

Evelyn Hope

EVELYN SAT IN HER office and tried to tell herself she wasn't worried. The team was on the hunt and they were well trained. They had every advantage in weapons and equipment and they would surely have the element of surprise. That had to count too, didn't it?

George was off doing whatever it was he did when he wasn't in her office, and that left her with only her thoughts for company.

Subject Seven was alive. She was still having trouble accepting that. Her hand reached for the necklace around her neck, once again playing with the wedding ring and bronzed tooth that rested against her skin. Her dead husband's wedding ring. Her first son's tooth. Bobby's tooth.

When Bobby first disappeared, he'd called her several times, and she'd always reacted the same way, sending out a group to locate him and bring him back. He'd never been there to meet with those teams. She'd long since accepted that he was dead—but now, after all this time, maybe he was alive after all.

Her hand clenched the necklace tightly, and she squeezed her tokens until she could feel the sharp sting of the tooth trying to break her skin.

Her free hand rested next to her phone.

She needed to be able to answer at a moment's notice. The Strike Team could call in and she wanted—*needed*—to know if they'd succeeded. The Strikers were good—fast and better trained than most standard-issue soldiers—but they were up against Subject Seven, and he had a history of violence that was unsettling.

She needed to know when they found Seven. Needed to know that the monster had been captured so that he could be brought back to her. She had given him clues, but there had been no contact as of yet. The Strikers were simply following the best route possible at this point.

He had so much to answer for.

The phone rang shrilly in her silent office, and she remained where she was, unflinching, until the third ring. There was no reason to be in a hurry and certainly no reason to let anyone know she was impatient for answers.

"Hello?"

It was Rafael. "We have them in sight."

Evelyn took a deep, slow breath and forced herself to stay calm.

"Bring them to me. Preferably alive. Call me when it's done."

"Yes, ma'am."

That was all he had to say. She knew he would obey.

It was what he was made to do, after all. Unlike Seven and the others with him, Rafael was a success.

Chapter Four

Kyrie Merriwether

THE FOOD SAT LIKE a lump in her stomach. She'd eaten because she had to, but it was hard to enjoy it with Hank sitting next to her. If she'd met him on the street and never known what he was, she would have had an easier time of it, she supposed. But knowing that he was the thing that hid inside of Cody—little, skinny Cody, who was so shy and sweet—made it harder to accept him. Hank seemed nice enough, but she knew better. If what they'd been told was true, and she had to assume it was, he was designed to be a killing machine. Maybe he had a nice attitude and maybe he was just trying to be nice until he decided it was time to start breaking necks.

Either way, he'd been staring her square in the chest for long enough to irritate her, and she had a headache from not telling him to put his eyes back in his head. Tina might have the chops to square off with him, but not her. Kyrie wasn't anywhere near as bold as the other girl in the group.

They climbed back into the car—Hank was too damned big to fit easily in the backseat so he was in the front passenger's seat instead, which left Kyrie feeling at least a little better. Kyrie sat with Tina on her left and Gene on her right. Hunter was driving, which was good. This way she could study him without him realizing it.

Hunter was good looking, no two ways about it. He was also quiet and very, very angry. She could feel his frustration like it was heat coming from an oven, low and simmering and ready to flare up at any time. And damned if she didn't find that edge of danger sexy as all get out. Hank scared the crap out of her and he was behaving himself, while Hunter was stiff and almost knotted with anger and she thought he was hot. Where was the logic in that? Not that it mattered. She couldn't let herself start falling for a guy she'd just met, especially since she didn't know how long she'd know any of them. She had a life to get back to, just as soon as they could find a way to stop their darker selves from emerging. Joe Bronx had summed it up pretty well when he'd pointed out that their Hydes had no concern about their families and Kyrie couldn't risk Not-Kyrie waking up and deciding she didn't like one of Kyrie's loved ones.

A shiver ran through her. She didn't know for certain

that her Other had killed anyone, but there was a very real chance. Kyrie didn't much like that idea. Not at all, actually. She was raised to believe in mercy and the values her family held as sacred. Killing was a sin. She was a good girl. If she died—if she managed to screw everything up and get herself killed before this was all resolved—what did that say about where she was going if her Other was a murderer? Kyrie believed in heaven and dreaded the thought of hell.

She shook her head, exasperated with herself and the mess her world had become, as the car pulled onto the interstate and started accelerating. When they left Boston, Joe Bronx had cruised down the road at seventy miles an hour. In comparison, his Other, Hunter, drove slower, more cautiously. He barely nudged the car up to sixty.

The road was almost empty except for their car. It was the timing, she supposed. They were in the middle of nowhere and the worst traffic would start later, when work began for the people who worked in the nine-to-five world.

She looked around, uncomfortable. When she woke up in the middle of Nebraska, she'd tried hitchhiking back to her home in Seattle, and that had ended poorly. Sometimes people expect a certain kind of payment for a ride and sometimes they'd get insistent.

Kyrie didn't like to think about what might have happened if her Other hadn't come to her rescue. It made her feel a little better about not knowing where the trucker (who'd been trying to get frisky) had vanished to. The radio talked again about the missing truckload of firearms. She tried not to dwell on the fact that the driver was missing too.

The truck? She knew where that was. It was in Boston, where she'd met up with the rest of the group. Somewhere along the way, it had been emptied of handguns and rifles and whatever else had been inside of it, courtesy of Joe Bronx, who also let Kyrie know that her Other had brought it along to the rendezvous.

She crossed her arms over her chest and shivered again. How was any of this possible? She was just a kid. She wasn't in a hurry to grow up; but here she was driving across the stupid country to find a woman who was supposed to make everything all better. Driving with a group of strangers who had more in common with her, physically, than she had with her family. She wanted it all to go away. She wanted to be home again. Was that even possible? Could she ever go back to her old life?

Kyrie had been raised in a Christian family. She went to church every Sunday and she took care of her brothers and sisters and she was a cheerleader and a dancer and a high school sophomore. She wasn't a gunrunner or a killer or a trained spy. Yet here she was, dealing with all of the insanity that had been dropped in her lap when Joe Bronx woke up the Other that was hiding inside of her.

Was that right? She frowned, uncertain. Did Joe have

something to do with what had happened to her? She wasn't sure. She couldn't be sure. She hadn't asked him, and he surely wasn't offering any information.

Joe Bronx. He was Hunter's other self. His Other. He was as different from Hunter as Hank was from Cody, and he was dangerous in the worst possible way. He was handsome, true, like Hunter, but so different that she could barely accept they were the same being. Bronx was smooth and confident and absolutely predatory. Every move he made was sleek and charged with restrained power. He didn't walk; he stalked. He didn't speak; he growled. His smile wasn't friendly; it was a baring of fangs, and yet he still managed to come across as both intelligent and fascinating. She didn't mind looking at Hunter—he was handsome enough. But she couldn't take her eyes off Joe Bronx when he was around. He was larger than life. She'd never understood that saying before she met him. He was fascinating and terrifying at the same time.

He scared her half to death.

Tina nudged her with an elbow and nodded toward Gene on her other side. Gene had gone to sleep, his eyes closed, his mouth hanging open, and was snoring softly. His arms were crossed tightly over his chest, and despite the fact that he was obviously sleeping, he looked rigid with tension.

She studied him silently for a second before lights started filling the car.

"What the hell?" Kyrie squinted against the sudden illumination.

She looked to the left and saw the bright headlights glaring into the side windows. Whatever was coming toward them was coming from the wrong direction and aiming for a collision.

"Hunter!"

The boy didn't answer her. He was already slamming on the old car's brakes and fighting with the steering wheel. Without a word Hank reached out and yanked the wheel toward him hard enough to take the car out of its skid and onto the shoulder. The vehicle that had been coming for them, that had almost smashed into them, rocketed past with a squeal of rubber and then straightened out and stopped behind them.

Hank's voice was a low, deadly growl. "Looks like we've got trouble." He was smiling as he spoke. "Sweet."

Hunter didn't reply. He was looking around, back at the van that had tried to ram them. The vehicle wasn't moving yet, but no one trusted it would just sit there after trying to hit them.

Hank opted not to wait around to find out. He opened the door of the car and slid out in one smooth step, rolling his shoulders and eyeing the van like it was a new victim.

Tina hollered after him, "Where do you think you're going? Get the hell back over here!"

Hank stood still. He didn't bother responding to Tina.

Kyrie shook her head while Gene looked around, just coming out of his daze. Hunter killed the engine and looked at Hank. "What the hell is he doing?"

Tina scowled. "I guess he's gonna try to eat that van. He's almost big enough."

The headlights on the other vehicle shut off, leaving all of them half blinded by the sudden darkness.

Hunter called out to Hank: "Either get back in here or go find out what the hell is wrong with that loser."

Hank leaned in closer, keeping his eyes on the van. "*Those* losers. There are six of them."

"How do you know?"

"I can smell 'em." He looked quickly at Hunter. "If you can make Joe show up, you might want to. I think we're about to be in really serious trouble here."

"How serious?"

"The kind that makes me wish I knew how to fire a gun."

Kyrie wished suddenly that Joe was there. Joe could have done something about this. At the very least he could have woken up Others.

Gene looked at Hank's massive figure. Taking a deep breath, he slid out of the car.

"Where are you going?" Tina's voice was sharp and a little worried.

Gene glanced her way and then gestured toward Hank

with his chin. "Someone's got to have his back."

Kyrie's heart was pounding, and her ears were starting to ring. She felt the panic eating away at her. She barely knew any of the people with her, but they were all in on this together. Her knees were shaking as she crawled toward the door and joined Gene and Hank on the asphalt.

Behind her, she heard Tina's voice calling out, "Don't just sit there, Hunter, get out of the damn car."

Kyrie didn't turn her head. She didn't bother looking, but she knew the other two were climbing out of the car too. A second later the latch on the trunk popped open.

The trunk, where the loaded guns were sitting.

Gene moved toward the trunk.

The lights on the other van flashed back on—they were blindingly bright.

Hank stepped forward, his savage grin returning. His expression was filled with dangerous glee.

He slammed his fist into the palm of his other hand. "Rock and roll. Let's dance."

Chapter Five

Gene Rothstein

GENE'S PULSE WAS SINGING in his veins, and his hands shook as he reached for the trunk. He knew exactly where to reach, because he was the one who'd checked the weapons and slipped them into secure spots. He grabbed a .38 caliber Smith & Wesson snub nose. It wasn't the prettiest weapon or the most intimidating, but it was loaded with one full clip of bullets—seventeen shots total. He didn't like the idea of firing a weapon. He didn't like any of what was going on. But he knew that anyone who'd tried to run them off the road was going to likely be the sort that carried firearms of his own.

Gene suddenly found himself wishing that his Other would show up. He knew he could fire a weapon. He knew if he had to, he could probably hit a target. What bothered him was the idea of actually shooting at a living human being.

The twitch in his hand was nerves. He told himself that was all it was but suspected it might mean something more. Maybe he was going to get his wish—maybe the Other that hid away inside of him was going to come out and take care of the dirty work for him. God, he hoped so.

Gene was used to a very different life. Most of the time his routine involved studying during school or dealing with the debate team after school (or the Chess Club, or half a dozen other extracurricular activities that were designed to prepare him for the future). This? No part of his former life resembled this. This was madness. This was insanity and delirium all rolled into one package, designed to make him feel too small for his skin.

The doors of the van rumbled open. Only one figure emerged, just outside the halo of light that streamed from the front of the van. Gene could barely see his body—forget clearly identifying the face.

"All of you need to calm down." The voice was deep and authoritative. Whoever he was, he was used to being obeyed.

Tina spit. "*You* need to stop running people off the road, asshole!"

Gene ignored her. He ignored the other speaker too. He was busy noticing the sort of detail that he always noticed. The van rocked slightly; the headlights shivered and shifted just a little. Not once or twice, but repeatedly. There was no rhythm to the changes, which meant it wasn't the engine that was causing them.

"They're spreading out," he said.

"Who are you?" Hunter called.

"We're here to help you." The voice that replied was calm, level.

"Who are you?" Hunter said again, sounding seriously stressed this time.

In the near complete darkness of the early morning a figure darted off to the far left, well beyond where Hank stood.

"Hank!" Gene pointed and the Other looked toward the darkness.

Hank sighed. "Yeah. I got it." He took two steps in that direction and then he bolted toward the shape Gene had seen, moving faster than anyone that big should have been able to.

The figure at the front of the van called out louder this time. "Which one of you is Bobby?"

"Who the hell is Bobby?" Tina's voice was tense, but still steady enough.

Another shape moved, this time to the far right. Gene took aim and called out, "Freeze! You come one step closer and I swear I'll shoot you!" His hand was steady, despite the way his knees were shaking. Adrenaline was pounding through him, making him light headed, but his father had taken him to gun safety and marksmanship courses enough times that he at least knew how to keep his hands from rattling as much as the rest of him.

The voice from in front of the the van called out, "Screw this. Take 'em!"

The lights shut off again, cloaking everyone in darkness. Gene's eyes had just adjusted to the brightness, and the sudden lack of light left him effectively blinded. He fired once at where the shape had been moving but heard no sound to indicate that he'd hit anything. Before he could fire a second time, a strong, feminine voice hissed in his ear, "You better watch what the hell you aim at."

Before he could so much as readjust his aim, the hands had grabbed him and he felt a leg sweep his legs. He was airborne and flipped over a lean, hard body a second after that. He yelped as he sailed through the air and then slammed into the ground. The impact rattled through him and knocked the wind from his lungs with an explosive *mmmf.*

As he tried to take in another breath, his unseen opponent kicked him in the wrist and sent his weapon spinning. Gene let out a yelp, then felt the same body land on top of him, a knee slamming into his solar plexus and stomach hard enough to make him gag.

"Got one!" The voice came from above him. He couldn't protest—couldn't argue—as the shadow rolled him easily onto his stomach and wrenched his hands behind his back. His hands were bound together a second later, a hard plastic line forcing them together. Gene grunted and gasped for breath, failing miserably.

"Big man got himself a gun." The voice hissed in his ear, then a fist cuffed him across the side of his head hard enough to make him see stars. "Loser."

In the distance someone let out a deep roar of pain and at the same time Gene heard Hank call out, "Try that again! I'll break your damned head!"

Tina let out a stream of obscenities and grunted a few times. It sounded like she was involved in a serious fight.

Somewhere else, Kyrie screamed.

Gene felt himself starting to fade, before the person he was fighting suddenly yanked him off the ground by his bound wrists. The pain was enough to make him whimper.

Then he heard Joe Bronx scream inside his head.

WAKE UP! WAKE UP!

And the world went away.

Chapter Six

Joe Bronx

TO GIVE CREDIT WHERE it was due, the loser had tried to do it the right way. Not that Joe was surprised to see Hunter fail. Hunter was soft, weak and easily confused by things like unexpected attacks.

Joe didn't have that problem. He'd been on the streets since the ripe old age of ten, and he'd run across every type of predator there was, from feral dogs to the sort of human trash that made the savages seem civilized. He knew how to handle animals.

Joe had been watching the whole thing. That was one of his advantages over Hunter. Joe didn't have to be in charge of their shared body to see what was happening. He'd learned a few tricks along the way and he'd been dominant for a very long time. He was capable of listening in on Hunter's life. That was a secret he intended to keep to himself.

Hunter had tried speaking with the people in the van. But he couldn't even see them—his senses were too limited. Off in the distance the only Other on the scene—Hank—was holding his own against a fighter that was trained and fast. Almost too fast.

Joe saw that Gene was down and out. The girl on him moved like a panther and slapped him senseless before he could even take a proper aim with his gun. Not that it would have done him any good. She was too close for firearms. Gene hadn't known that, of course, thought Joe. He'd probably been trying to see past the lights on the van. Hunter had been smart enough not to look at the lights, but most people looked automatically; like moths heading for a flame, their eyes were drawn to the brightness.

And while Hunter had been watching Gene get knocked senseless, Joe had taken advantage of the situation and forced control over their shared body. Hunter had fought, of course, but he'd been too distracted to realize he was in trouble before it was too late. Hunter still didn't understand how it worked. Joe was the dominant force within them. He could probably hold the little bastard at bay forever, if he didn't need to sleep same as anyone else in the world. He'd rested now, while Hunter tried to force his way through to Illinois instead of resting himself. Taking over had been easy.

And when Joe came out, he woke the Others.

That was a good thing, because he was pretty sure that what they were dealing with were more Doppelgangers. Different from them, of course, because these Others had been trained. They were too fast to be human, too young to be soldiers, and too well armed to be a street gang. Street gangs didn't carry zip strips for handcuffing their enemies. Street gangs didn't carry Tasers and heavy artillery.

He and his associates were Failures. These were the Successes.

And they were working together too well. They were clearly used to it. And one last thing: there wasn't a radio among them that Joe could see, but they had broken in different directions and circled their enemies without so much as a yelled command.

The voices of the Others rang in Joe's head and he grinned. Joe and his associates were the castoffs. When they'd been discarded, they were thought to be merely human. They might not work the way they should, but they still got the job done.

He looked around, taking in the details of his surroundings in an instant.

Not-Kyrie let out a growl and drove her knee into the face of her attacker. He fell back, cursing, as blood exploded from his busted lips and nose. He'd been expecting a fight with a little cheerleader, not with an Other. They were trained, but he would have bet all their stolen mob money that their enemies were not used to fighting against other Doppelgangers.

Not-Tina was being held in a full-nelson maneuver, with her attacker's hands locked behind her neck and both of her arms captured within the arms of the woman holding her. By all rights she should have been stuck, her useless arms held away from her body while her attacker held all the cards. It might have worked that way, too, but the change in her shape and size had thrown her Success a bit and loosened the fierce grip she'd had.

As Joe looked on, wondering if he should help, Not-Tina lifted one foot and drove her heel backward along the length of her enemy's shin and then into the top of the uniformed girl's foot. The sudden attack caught the soldier off guard, and as she tried to recover from the unexpected, searing pain in her leg, Not-Tina drove her head back, smashing the girl in her face.

"Lost your mind? I'll kill you!" Not-Tina was furious. All of the frustration that Tina had been feeling had been distilled and concentrated into her Other, and Not-Tina was hardly the sort to tolerate being treated wrongly. The fight was on fast and hard between the two of them, with the other girl going on the defensive as Not-Tina lashed out with wild, brutal punches.

Joe could have called for her to control herself—too

much anger would make her sloppy, and she wasn't skilled enough as a fighter to survive that—but she seemed to be holding her own for the moment.

He looked toward Not-Gene, who had just finished his transformation. The female that had been on him was crouched down low to the ground and studying him. Her eyes were wide open and her pupils glowed in the faint light like a cat's. She did not attack, though she assessed what had happened to her target. Gene's Other was larger and darker than Gene. He was also calmer than Not-Tina. While Not-Tina was swinging wildly, Not-Gene looked at his enemy with an almost serene expression on his face. The plastic that had cuffed his wrists together had broken as he grew larger. A fine line of blood dribbled down both his wrists as he stared at the girl and shook out his hands, forcing blood back to his extremities.

Finally the girl moved on him, charging forward. Gene didn't strike her, but instead he slid to the side, farther from the car and the girl. She pursued, a smile forming on her face. Unlike Joe, she couldn't see what was on Not-Gene's mind, or she wouldn't have been smiling.

Joe took a second to see that, as he suspected, one of the other team was as motionless as him. He allowed himself a small smile. There it was, giveaway. The other observer was doing the same thing as he was, watching how his people acted and assessing the enemy. Probably that one was an Alpha.

The second time his enemy pounced, Not-Gene let her hit him and the two of them fell farther away from the car still, with her on top of him again. She was a good fighter—well trained—but she was also cocky. She wasn't used to fighting anyone with the same sort of physical advantages that she had.

She also forgot to look where the gun she'd kicked from Gene's hand had landed. Not-Gene wasn't that careless.

Even as Not-Gene's hand clutched at the pistol, the apparent leader of the other team did the math in his head. Like Joe, he'd been watching and assessing, and now he turned quickly. "Mary! Back up, now!"

Without hesitation the girl did as told, flipping herself back and away from Not-Gene even as he spun and fired. The bullet barely missed blowing her head from her shoulders.

Not-Gene stood up in one smooth motion, keeping the weapon sited on the girl. She wasn't looking anywhere near as calm anymore.

The roar that came from the darkness surprised everyone, even Joe. He'd let himself focus too much on Not-Gene and, in the process, had let himself forget about Hank and the enemy that he was fighting.

Hank was the biggest of them, surely the most muscular, and he let out a roar as he charged toward the van. At first Joe thought that the brute had somehow grown even larger.

He was mistaken. The bulk that had been added to his running form was another of the soldiers who had engaged them. This one was trapped in Hank's arms and struggled madly to get free. Hank drove his enemy into the side of the van with enough force to rock the vehicle onto two wheels. Had he pushed any harder, the entire thing would have come down on its side. The sound of the impact was like thunder. Metal crumbled and bones snapped. And the calm leader who'd been looking at Joe as intently as Joe had been looking at him suddenly focused on the side of the van. "Sean!"

Joe had to guess Sean was the slab of meat Hank had just brutalized. Hank came back into view, his face bloodied and bruised, his eyes darkly murderous. Though Joe had no idea exactly what had happened, he could tell that Hank had been in a savage battle. He pounded his fist into the side of the van farthest away from Joe, doubtless hammering the face of his enemy again.

The dark-haired leader from the Successes met Joe's eyes. A grin pulled at the corners of Joe's mouth. He knew this one. They'd met in Boston.

Joe pulled the pistol from the seat of his running pants—Hunter had been a good boy and stowed a pistol in close range in the car—and aimed it at the other Alpha's head. But before he could pull the trigger, his target slid toward the van, vanishing from Joe's sight.

And then they were all moving, all of the enemies. They said nothing as they moved, but they stopped facing off and retreated at a fast pace.

"Hey! Bitch!" Not-Gene's voice exploded just before he triggered another explosion, this time from his pistol. The girl who'd been fighting him grunted and fell against the van's side, bleeding from her shoulder. "Something to remember me by!"

The van roared to life even as the other team was climbing into it. Joe could just see the shape of one of theirs being gently lifted into the vehicle. He aimed at the driver's side of the windshield and a few feet away, Not-Gene aimed as well.

Go for it. He sent the mental command toward Not-Gene, who silently nodded and blew out the windshield with a bullet. Joe could see the driver dropping even lower as he hit the gas and the van lurched forward, rapidly gathering speed. Hank slammed into the side of the moving vehicle, but the driver managed to keep his calm enough to compensate for the brutal impact.

Joe also fired, pounding holes into the vehicle, but his shots failed to hit a single target inside the damned thing. He could hear them screaming in furious, panicked voices. The sounds did him good.

Hank watched the retreating van and a slow smile worked its way across his brutish features. He'd just been in a knock-down, drag-out fight with someone mean enough to make him bleed, and he seemed amused by the notion. Not far away, Not-Tina was screaming obscenities and all but snarling. Not-Kyrie was almost as bad, flexing her hands and shaking off the fight. Not-Gene very calmly checked his pistol's clip and, on realizing it was empty, moved toward the car.

"Well, that was unexpected." Joe spoke softly, but they all listened to him. That was the way it was supposed to be. He was their leader, whether or not they liked it, or even knew it. His eyes cut to Hank, who'd stood up to him the last time they were both in charge of their bodies. Even Hank was his subordinate, despite his display of power the previous night. Joe remembered watching the Other crush the pistol in his hand, a feat Joe could not match on his best day. Hank could have killed Joe. He'd had the weapon aimed at Joe's head and instead had settled for a display of power and a warning. Hank just wanted his privacy. Joe would respect that. For now.

Not-Gene had walked to the back of the battered old car they were driving in and was sorting through a suitcase. He pulled out a box of ammunition and began reloading his clip. The others came closer, regrouping. Of the whole lot the one who looked the worst for wear was Hank, who was once again rolling his shoulders and looking toward where the van had gone. The van had headed down the road toward Illinois and Chicago.

"Who the hell were they?" Not-Gene's voice was still surprisingly calm

Joe shook his head. "I have no idea. But I think maybe we got the attention of the wrong people. I think they were like us. Others."

Not-Tina nodded. "They are. Too fast to be human. Too damn tough, too. I hit that bitch hard enough to break her jaw, but she kept coming."

Not-Kyrie added her own opinion. "They smelled like us."

That caught Joe's attention. "How do we smell?"

She frowned. "Not like people. Different. I don't think I can put it into words."

Not-Gene finished reloading and slid the pistol into his belt, carefully setting the safety first. "Whoever they are, they got stupid."

Not-Gene was getting cocky. Joe needed to correct that.

"No." Joe shook his head. "We got lucky. I don't think they were expecting us to change. If I hadn't taken over from Hunter, we would've been screwed. They were better trained than us. They had weapons and they were used to working together."

"Like I said. They got stupid. They weren't expecting us to change and they challenged us. They'd been smart about it, they would have just shot us and been done with it."

"They didn't use any weapons. They didn't want to hurt us." Not-Tina was finally calming down a bit, but she was still looking everywhere. Her counterpart was used to being paranoid as a result of growing up in a very violent neighborhood, and that had apparently carried over when she changed.

Hank laughed. "Could have fooled me. Bastard tried to throat me." He pointed to the red mark on his thick neck. All of them saw the abrasion easily, but only because they were enhanced and the darkness around them wasn't as much of a handicap for them. Had they been merely human, their senses would have failed them. Except maybe for Kyrie. Kyrie seemed a little better at seeing and hearing than the rest of the Failures. Maybe not quite as sharp-sensed as her counterpart, but better than human. He would have to test that theory, when he had the time.

"No. She's right. If they'd really wanted us dead, they would have just opened fire. All of them were carrying. They could have just cut loose and blown us to hell. They want us alive."

"So what does that mean?" Not-Gene was frowning, not upset so much as trying to figure out the angles of this particular equation. It was what he did. He liked to understand what was behind the actions of all the people around him. He liked the puzzles of human minds. Joe could admire that. He also looked at the other Failure's analytical mind as a possible risk that had to be considered.

"It means they probably got sent after us by Janus. That means we might not be able to surprise Evelyn Hope the way we wanted to."

"So what? We're screwed?" Not-Tina's voice rose as she spoke. Joe suppressed a desire to tell her to calm down. It wouldn't do any good. She was high-strung, and it would just rile her even more.

"No. We just have a few new obstacles." That was Hank. He looked at Joe for a second with a strange smile on his face and then he looked toward Not-Tina. "They don't want us dead. They just want us. For all we know, if those losers had caught us, they'd have taken us where we want to go, to see Evelyn Hope."

"Not a chance in hell." Joe shook his head violently. "We might have gotten there, but we wouldn't be in any position to fight back."

"How do you know that?" Not-Gene again. Not challenging him, just curious. It was good to be able to sense what they were thinking. It made worrying about betrayal unnecessary. Of course, there was Hank to consider too. Hank knew Joe could read their thoughts, could feel it when he read them. He had to avoid even seriously considering messing with Hank for the present time, and that was inconvenient.

"Because I was their unfortunate guest, remember? I told

you before, you guys had your lives as regular people. I had a life of getting experimented on."

"Why doesn't Hunter remember any of that?" Not-Kyrie. She was looking at Joe with a puzzled frown. "What did they do to him?"

They hadn't done anything to Hunter. A collision with a car had brained Hunter hard enough to destroy his memories, his ability to exist, for several years. Now he was coming back around, which was why Seven had started hunting down the rest of the Failures in the first place. That was where the problems began, wasn't it? That was the source of most of his frustration. Trying to find a cure for his dilemma had led him to discover that there were other Failures out there and that, in turn, had led the lot of them to where they were now. He just couldn't explain that to the others, not yet at any rate. Not until he was sure exactly who he could trust and how well he could trust them. Maybe not even then.

"I don't know. Look, I know some of you have bleed over. Some of you can remember your other selves." He looked at Hank and Not-Gene, both of whom had shown certain signs of the syndrome. "I don't. I can't remember what Hunter does. I have to guess. It hasn't exactly made this easy for me. Or for him, I guess." This wasn't exactly the truth, but it was close enough for Joe's purposes.

Hank stared hard at him, a smile playing around his

mouth again. Joe was tempted to check what was going on in that head but knew if he did, Hank would do to him what he had done to the van and the soldier he'd used to dent it. Hank was on an entirely different level than the other Failures strength-wise. Joe thought he could probably still take him, but not without getting seriously damaged in the process.

That meant waiting until the right time to test out his theories. There was something about Hank that bothered Joe a lot. More than just his challenging nature. How had he realized that Joe was reading his mind? Why did it seem sometimes that maybe Hank was returning the favor? These weren't thoughts that Joe liked very much.

"I don't know who those losers were, and I don't much care. What I do know is we have to go faster if we're going to get to Evelyn Hope. Climb in, kiddies. We have a mission to finish."

Without another word he headed for the car. The others followed. He knew they would. They didn't fit as well as they should have. All of them were bigger than in their other forms. In the long run, Not-Tina wound up sitting in Hank's lap. Hank didn't complain. Neither did Not-Tina, who enjoyed being the center of attention more than her counterpart did.

Chapter Seven

Not-Gene

THE RADIO WAS PLAYING in the car, and as much as he hated country music, he listened to the words of the songs playing. He knew the singer, of course. The man was a legend, even if he was dead. Johnny Cash—that was the name. He knew it because Gene's father liked to listen to the man when he was working in the garage, or at least pretending to work in the garage. Gene's "dad," the man who had raised him as a son, also listened to the nonsense whenever he was hunting or off pretending to be a man with his college friends. Football games, the occasional sports outing, whatever let him have freedom from the harpy he'd married. Gene loved his mother, admired her greatly, even when he was angry with her like he was now. Not-Gene didn't much care for her either way. She was neither good nor bad, but merely another person in the world.

The song was about a man going to his death, unrepentant, unforgiving and unafraid. That was something he could admire, and so he smiled and nodded.

"You said we should name ourselves?" He spoke to Joe. Not quite asking permission but merely asking for clarification.

The man who liked to think of himself as their leader nodded. "Absolutely. You're all going to need names when it comes time for fake IDs. Why? You come up with something?"

He smiled. "Yeah. Call me Sam Hall."

Bronx smiled. "Like the song?"

"Definitely."

Bronx laughed. "Good one! Sam Hall it is, 'damn your eyes!'"

Sam nodded, acknowledging the line from the song. Seemed about the only thing Sam Hall in the song liked to say, really. And it suited exactly how Sam felt about most of the people in the world around him. The Others, maybe even the Failures, they were a bit different. They were kin. There was a connection to them that went beyond the link that let Joe speak to them through their minds. There was a camaraderie that came from being almost unique in this world.

Not like the others, the ones that wanted to take their freedom from them.

Sam smiled. "Damn your eyes, indeed." He said the words softly as he thought about the girl who'd damned near beaten Gene unconscious. He would finish what he started with her if he saw her again. The more he thought about the girl, the more she enraged him. It didn't seem to work that way with all of them. Not everyone felt offended when someone hurt their counterparts, but he did. And so did Hank. He was fairly sure of it.

He was connected with Gene. He didn't much like that fact, but he understood it. The worst part was he didn't much like Gene. Hank seemed to accept Cody, maybe even sort of liked him, but Sam didn't feel that way at all when it came to his counterpart. Gene was weak. He held everything inside and took whatever was thrown his way like it was something that he deserved. Like he had to be punished for having a life of privilege. Sam didn't know for sure if that was how Gene felt, but he suspected it was. He wasn't Gene. He shared some memories, and he sometimes felt the emotions that Gene was feeling, but he wasn't really connected beyond that. What made Gene angry made him angry; he understood that too. But it was different for Hank and even for the two females. So far when they changed, they took on the same emotions as their Jekylls, but none of the memories. He could tell by the way they looked around when the transformation occurred. They were disoriented, but in the case of Tina, he could see the fury whenever she became Not-Tina. She came into the world enraged every single time. Of course there was little to go on for that. So far he'd only seen her become Not-Tina a few times and normally he was busy waking up himself.

That was something he and Gene had in common: they studied everything around them. They wanted to know everything. The difference? Gene wanted to hide from the things that scared him, wanted to hide from the aspects of his own personality that worried him. Sam wanted to embrace everything. There was so very much he hadn't done yet.

Kyrie sat next to him, looking out the window, lost in thought. In the front seat, Hank rode shotgun with Not-Tina in his lap and Joe drove, turning off the interstate and heading onto a side road without consulting any maps.

Joe had been around for five years. It was impossible to imagine how much he had already experienced. Sam envied him every last second of his life.

"Where are we going?" He asked the question just to see what Joe would say. He didn't really much care, as long as he could be alive, be in existence, instead of giving control back to Gene. But he wanted to know more about Joe, more about the guy who was basically in charge of their lives right now.

Joe looked at him in the rearview mirror, his dark blue eyes unreadable. "I think we need to stretch our legs for a bit." He shrugged. "I know we need to get to a certain destination, but first we need to make a plan and for that I need to think. And I think best when I'm moving. So, let's move."

As he spoke he pulled off the road and into the parking lot of a sleazy-looking bar. There were several trucks there already and half a dozen motorcycles that had been tricked out enough to guarantee they belonged to a bike club. Bike club, like Hell's Angels was a bike club. Hardly a mild little social group.

Joe was out of the car before the engine finished settling, pocketing the keys and stretching his legs. Hank stood up and stretched, rolling his shoulders again. He was always doing that, and Sam had to wonder if the Other was having trouble adjusting to the size change that his body had to go through each time. That was something to consider for the future. Gene would have noticed the same thing, but the difference was, Sam noticed it and cataloged it for later.

The rest of them climbed out and Sam couldn't help looking at the two girls. Both of them had grown when they changed from Jekyll to Hyde. They'd grown larger. The end result was clothing that strained in the most interesting areas. Not-Kyrie looked around with a smile playing on her lips and moved forward with a sensual strut that was completely unconscious. Kyrie seemed almost self-conscious about her looks. Not-Kyrie reveled in the knowledge that men were looking. She exuded confidence that bordered on arrogance. Not-Tina was on the prowl. That was the only way to put it. Every move she made was fluid grace, and the expression on her face was purely predatory. Not necessarily in a good way for whatever she decided to stalk, either. She was attractive, yes, but there was a serious edge of danger to her. Not surprising, not really, not when you considered that she had apparently taken a couple of million dollars from mobsters in New Jersey. Sam decided to keep that in mind, just in case he found himself alone with her again. They'd fought alongside each other on the very first occasion when they met, and while he knew that his body was physically stronger and more durable than Gene's, Not-Tina had recovered from being hit with a Taser faster than he had. It was possible that she was tougher than he was, and that said a lot.

Still, he looked at the way the two of them wore their now tighter pants and it wasn't combat he thought of. A flash of a smile played across his face as the group headed into the bar. Well, not combat, but definitely something just as physical.

Chapter Eight

Joe Bronx

THE PLACE WAS A dump, just like he remembered. Not-Tina slid a hand over his bicep and moved in front of him. She wanted to be seen—to be acknowledged—so for a moment he saw her. She was easy to look at. Tina was a rail, thin and pretty, yes, but not exactly stunning. Not-Tina was sleek muscles and had the same sort of appeal as a panther. Unsettling and deadly but absolutely impossible to ignore.

"How do you know this place?" Her voice had the same strong New Jersey accent as Tina's, but otherwise everything was different. They didn't speak with the same rhythms or use the same words. Different bodies and different minds in one form; each of the Others was developing, becoming a complete individual, and it was fascinating to watch.

Joe smiled and placed a hand on her shoulder, making sure to look into her eyes deeply. It was what she wanted, intimacy, and he needed all of them on his side. "I've been all around. Been to Chicago about ten times before. I found this place a couple of years ago."

This place was Mark-O's Bar. He had yet to meet anyone named Mark in the place. He didn't go looking, either. It had cheap beer, decent food and no particular worry about carding or checking IDs, so it was good enough for Joe's purposes.

The others quickly found a table that had just been emptied. Hank eyed the mess left behind and then started picking up the beer mugs and dirty dishes. Rather than bother with the work herself, Not-Kyrie caught the eye of a heavyset waitress and gestured for her to do it. The waitress moved quickly, a nervous expression on her face, and began busing the table.

Not-Tina reached into her pocket and pulled a handful of quarters from inside. She didn't bother explaining; instead she headed for the cubbyhole near the restrooms that had two pay phones. Even in a time when almost everyone carried cell phones, you could still find a few pay phones if you looked hard enough. Joe risked a quick touch of her mind, just enough to skim over her intent, and realized that she was planning to call on the mob connections she had robbed on his behalf. Probably she wanted to play with them some more. Not-Tina seemed to like playing with her food.

Hunter wouldn't have approved. Hunter was all about being peaceful and happy and letting the sunshine in. At least he liked to tell himself that. In his defense, Hunter was suffering from amnesia, to Joe's perpetual joy. Back when Seven had been a lab rat, Hunter had been Bobby, a good little boy who was raised by loving parents and given a good upbringing. It was the bleed over of Bobby's happy memories into his tortured existence that had convinced Subject Seven to escape the labs in the first place. Now Bobby was called Hunter because he didn't know any better and Seven called himself Joe Bronx because he needed a name other than Subject Seven to answer to. No matter how much the world changed or the names shifted, one thing remained the same: Seven hated Hunter and always would.

The rest of them sat down and Joe ordered wings and a pitcher of beer. Maybe in a lot of places they would have asked for ID, but not at Mark-O's. If you had cash, they sold you what you wanted. That was why he'd chosen the place, and that much at least had not changed.

Hank was checking out a girl wearing enough leather to upholster the entire room. Joe couldn't blame him. She was attractive enough in a trashy way. She was also very obviously with a biker who was covered with tattoos and wearing the colors of the Road Kings, a biker gang that had charters in every state from New York to North Dakota.

"Keep staring at that, and her boyfriend might take it

personally." Joe's voice was amused, but also carried a warning. They weren't here to fight with anyone. They were too close to their goals.

"I could take him." Hank's voice was low, but his confidence was high.

"He's got friends."

Hank finally looked his way. "I could take them too."

"Probably true, but we can't afford the trouble."

Hank opened his mouth to say something, but before he could, Not-Kyrie slid onto his lap and ran her fingers through his thick hair. "Don't waste your eyes on that trash." Joe made sure not to look into Hank's thoughts, but Not-Kyrie was almost an open book. She was distracting Hank on purpose to defuse the tension she sensed between him and Joe.

Joe smiled tightly for her. He appreciated the assist, though he could have handled it himself. He also stifled the instant jealousy he felt; he had already decided he wouldn't allow himself to get to know either of the girls he was traveling with too well. He couldn't afford the complications that would come from it. He needed everyone on his side for now, and that meant he couldn't get personal with either of the girls because the other might take it as an insult. Politics. That was one thing about being on his own: he'd never had to worry about making nice in order to keep the peace.

Hank slid a possessive arm around Not-Kyrie's waist and

pulled her in closer. The waitress set down the pitcher and five mugs, and at the same time Sam looked over toward where Not-Tina was talking urgently into the phone.

"So what's up?" Hank spoke softly, very obviously distracted by the girl in his lap.

Joe resisted the temptation to answer that particular question bluntly, but Not-Kyrie smirked.

"As soon as Not-Tina gets back, we'll talk about it. Mostly I think we need to discuss the people we ran into earlier."

"They were hunting us." Sam's voice was calm. His face was troubled, but his posture and tone were controlled. He was making himself stay as composed as possible. Joe understood. The fight earlier had gotten his blood up, and he hadn't even really been involved much beyond watching. It was in their nature: they were quite literally designed to be killing machines, aggressive and quick to respond to challenges.

Not-Tina sat down and grabbed the pitcher, pouring herself a beer before she bothered to acknowledge anyone at all. She was smiling, excited. Whatever she'd been talking about on the phone had left her pleasantly agitated. Her eyes shone with mischief.

"What was that all about?" Joe tried to keep his tone light, but it wasn't easy. She could cause them trouble if she was playing games with the wrong people.

"Just had to say hello to some friends." She smiled, but the expression didn't reach her eyes. She wanted her privacy. Too bad. Joe reached into her mind again to see if he could glean anything. Her defenses were up. She wanted to keep something a secret, which by itself was enough to tell him that there were likely to be problems.

Joe saw Hank look his way as he tried to reach into Not-Tina's mind. He knew, but he didn't say anything. He merely got that little knowing, annoying half smile on his face for a moment as he looked at Joe.

Joe couldn't read their minds, not in the truest sense of the phrase. He could collect feelings sometimes, and he could now and then pull an image from them, but mostly the mental connection he had with the others was more like an assessment of their intentions. He'd scared Cody Laurel half to death with that ability by discussing things on the phone that he shouldn't have been able to see—things that were happening to Cody almost six hundred miles away. That had been a monumental effort, but it had been worth it because he'd convinced Cody to come to him in Boston with his ability to know more than he should have.

Unfortunately for him, Not-Tina was giving nothing away.

Sam tapped the table. "Okay, so let's talk about the losers who were trying for us earlier."

Joe looked his way. "I think they were like us, Others.

And I don't think they're done with us, not by any stretch. They didn't come after us to lose. They came after us to finish what we started in Boston."

Not-Tina nodded and spoke. "So what are we gonna do about them?"

Joe smiled. "Well now, I think that's where this could get interesting."

"Spill it." Hank poured himself a beer, drinking it like water despite the thick foam. Joe suppressed a desire to swat Hank. The more he was around him the less he liked him. He'd have to watch that.

"We're here because of a letter. That letter is almost guaranteed to be a setup. Think about it. The letter just happens to be the only paper left in the office where we got attacked. It also just happens to mention the only name I know for certain: Evelyn Hope. And it gives us her address and it gives us another name too."

"Wait. What other name?" Not-Tina was interrupting now too. He'd have to work on teaching them manners, but not right now. It could wait.

"Josh Warburton. Near as I can tell, he's one of the higher-ups. I figure if we can't use Evelyn Hope, he's the other possibility, but not as good a choice because he doesn't have an address on here.

"And the ones who tried to stop us? They have to work for Evelyn. They were too much like us for it to be a coincidence. They were looking for us, or else why would they have come along and stopped us in the middle of nowhere?"

Not-Tina shrugged and leaned back in her seat, her eyes looking over Hank and Not-Kyrie with an expression that was just a little too casual to be sincere. It obviously bothered her that the guys were flocking to the other girl more than to her, even if she didn't say anything about it. And that was why Joe was making himself behave around both of them for now. It would be too easy to get caught up in something messy. "Maybe he's dumb enough to be in the phone book," she said.

Joe shrugged. "Maybe. But let's worry about the rest of this first. This whole thing is a setup. Those guys either followed us from Boston, or they knew we were coming here, or they were sent to meet us here. Whatever the case, everything here smells like a trap." He stopped talking as the waitress set down a massive pile of wings. Not-Tina attacked them. Joe reached and grabbed one himself, sucking all the meat away from the bones before he continued. "What we need to do is go after what we were after all along. We just have to be aware that there are new players."

Sam shook his head. "What exactly are we after?"

"Freedom from the Others."

"And how are we going to get that?" Sam was interrupting now too. It was like a stupid question conspiracy. Still, he had to remind himself that the people he was dealing with were basically newborns. They had feelings and thoughts, yes, but they hadn't been conscious of the world around them until he made them aware of it. They were like little kids who wanted answers to everything, and he'd teach them restraint soon enough, at least the ones who lived through it all.

"Evelyn Hope. She made us. That means she has the answers. And if she doesn't have the answers, she knows where to get them. She's luring us back, obviously. She wants us there." Joe stared hard at Sam and then reached for another wing. "And if they've got others like us out there and fighting, then they've got more answers than I was hoping for." He smiled. "Wait and see. We're going to come out on top of this one."

Chapter Nine

Not-Tina

NOT-TINA LOOKED AT Joe and did her best to listen to his words, but it wasn't easy. She was still reflecting on the conversation she'd just finished with Paulo Scarabelli. Old Paulo, he wasn't in a very good mood.

She liked it that way.

He'd made a few threats, promised to kill her family, to make her pay for every dollar she'd stolen. And she'd listened, nodding all the way. Finally, when he was done making his threats and calling her a dozen names that would have shamed most women, Not-Tina spoke so softly, he had to strain to hear her.

She said, "I know where you live. I know your wife's name and I know your daughter. You hear me? I know little Annabelle, and if I ever hear you call me any of those names again, you fat pig, I'm gonna gut your little cow daughter and send her fat, rotting heart to your wife."

And as soon as he started screaming at her again, she hung up the phone.

She wasn't done with him. Not a chance. Maybe Tina wasn't ready for payback, but she was. Scarabelli was going to suffer a great deal at her hands, and then he was going to die for every slight he'd thrown against Tina and against her. What he'd done to Tina mattered, because it was part of what Not-Tina knew about the way the world worked. Best way to get what you want? Take it. Fat Paulo had taught her that and he didn't even know it.

She had a lot to thank him for. She was making lists and checking them off every time Tina went to sleep and she was freed.

Joe finished his opening speech. No two ways about it, the boy liked to hear himself speak. She was okay with that; he was still a nice-looking piece of eye-candy, and he was still working toward a goal they all wanted.

"Don't keep us in suspense." Hank was grinning, taking her in. She didn't mind. She sort of liked the attention. It made her happy to know that men looked at her with hunger while they basically ignored Tina. "Tell us about this plan of yours." Not-Kyrie was sitting firmly in his lap and Not-Tina could tell he was excited, but Hank was looking at her anyway. He had an appetite, that one. He wanted everything, maybe even more than she did. He'd woken himself up earlier. Maybe if she was lucky, he could teach her to do that too. So far the only time she got out to play was when Joe woke her when Tina was sleeping, or when Tina got good and scared. Really scared.

Joe Bronx nodded. "We know they want us. Probably they want to take us to the closest facilities where they can finish what they started with me and maybe look the rest of you over before they start chopping us into pieces."

"Why would they do that?" Not-Gene—no, Sam. He wanted to be called Sam—spoke, frowning again. He always had that look on his face, like he was puzzled and needed to know all the answers. Well, except when he looked like he wanted to kill something. She liked him better when he was pissed off. He was sexier that way.

"Like I said, we're the Failures. I was used for study, probably to help them figure out how to make the losers that came after us. You were thrown away. You shouldn't be alive and you shouldn't be able to change, so of course they want to know why you're still alive and what you can do."

Not-Tina nodded. "Lab rats. Wanna see if anything we can do would make the next group better."

"Exactly." Joe flashed her a smile. Too damned good looking for his own good.

"Too bad for them. I don't feel like getting cut up." Not-Tina looked around the room. There were a dozen guys in leather around the bar and a couple of skanks hanging all over them. They weren't all that bad looking—she'd certainly seen worse-looking guys—but they also acted like they owned the world. Long before she let any of them touch her, she'd have to teach them how to bathe.

"Here's the thing. I'm almost certain the address I have for Evelyn Hope is a plant. They wanted us to find it. I just think they got impatient and tried to get to us before we could get to that address. So we have to fix that. We have to go into the place ready for them. I mean locked, loaded, and ready to blow the hell out of whatever gets in our way." Joe's voice was low. He wasn't stupid enough to talk about shootings in a loud voice. Maybe the others were ignorant, but Not-Tina understood that every dive had the possibility of being a trap. Maybe it was a biker bar that didn't care about carding or maybe half the people at Mark-O's were actually working as informants. They couldn't be too safe.

She sipped at her beer again. The stuff was already half flat and tasted like horse piss. "Think maybe a few of us could use training, slick? I'm just sayin', I know the basics, but I've never had any formal training."

Joe smiled at her. "Here I thought you preferred the up-close and personal approach."

She shrugged. "So maybe I do, but that doesn't mean I want to go into anywhere without the right equipment."

Joe pointed at Sam. "We'll go over that after we

leave here. Right now we need to make sure everyone understands their part of this plan."

"What's to know? We shoot them first."

Joe smiled then, a broad unpleasant expression that looked like he was ready to rip out someone's throat.

"Not quite. No, I have something a little different in mind."

"Like what?" Sam again, still frowning. His eyes were glued to Not-Tina's chest, so she squared her shoulders to make sure he could get a better view.

Joe smiled. "We scope the place out, then we come back on our timetable and we take down anything that gets in our way. They know we have weapons, but they don't know that we're all going to know how to use those weapons by tomorrow."

Hank managed to look up from his close scrutiny of Not-Kyrie long enough to let them know he was actually listening. "Who's gonna teach us?"

"Sam. Sam has a lot of practice. We're going to learn tonight, before we go to sleep."

"How?" Not-Kyrie wrinkled her brow when she asked the question. Not-Tina rolled her eyes. Even the girl's confused look exuded sex appeal.

"It's the way we're designed. We were made to learn fast, especially when I'm here to allow a mental connection. It's kind of like computers. We'll download the information directly from Sam's head."

Sam's frown got bigger. "Wait. You're going to get into my head? What if I don't want that?"

Chapter Ten

Evelyn Hope

EVELYN HELD HERSELF IN check, though it was an effort. She did not like being kept waiting, didn't appreciate not knowing the answers to questions she needed answered. She knew George was working on getting everything taken care of, but still, patience was a virtue that she had little desire to pursue at the moment.

George was in the room, working away on tracking down information on the four unknown entities that were running around with Subject Seven. He was smart enough to keep quiet. George could read her like a book, which was one of the reasons she kept him around. It was hard to find good help. As if to prove her point, the phone rang harshly. George flinched at the unexpected noise. She did not.

She answered the phone immediately; Caller ID had told her all she needed to know. "Do you have them?"

"No, ma'am. They got away." Did he sound worried? Yes, he did, with very good reason.

"Would you care to explain that to me, Rafael? Would you like to clarify for me exactly how five unprepared targets got away from the best of my soldiers?" Her tone was frigid.

"They were stronger than we expected." His voice cracked a bit and she reminded herself that he was young, only thirteen despite his size and training. "Sean was badly hurt."

"Am I hearing tears now, Rafael?"

His voice tightened up instantly and she could almost hear him standing straighter. "No, ma'am!"

"How badly was he hurt?" Sean was a good boy, a good fighter, and normally careful to not get injured.

"He's got a concussion and a few broken bones. Whoever hit him, he was like a rhino." There was a pause, but she sensed there was more.

"What else?"

"Mary took a bullet in the shoulder."

"And?"

"She's recovering, just meat, no bone struck, but she lost a good amount of blood."

Evelyn's lips pressed together and she looked toward George, who was eavesdropping exactly as she would have expected him to. Without a word spoken, he walked across her office to the bar and began pouring her two fingers of scotch. She wasn't much of a drinker, but now and then she needed something to help her relax.

"Did they suffer any injuries?" Her fingers sought her tokens again, the reminders of her past.

"No. They got away." She could hear the frustration in his voice.

"So." She nodded. "Get them. Either get them at the address I provided or before then."

"Yes, ma'am."

"And Rafael?"

"Ma'am?"

"Do I have to express how disappointed I'll be if you fail me twice?"

"It won't happen a second time, ma'am."

"Good boy." She took a sip of her drink and let the heat wash through her before she spoke again. "Now then, one last thing."

"Whatever you need, Ms. Hope."

"When you see them, I need you to say something for me; I need you to yell it out."

"What's that?"

"Say it exactly as I do, understood?"

"Of course."

She spoke the words and made him repeat it twice to be sure.

After the call was over, she placed the scotch on the desk in front of her and steepled her fingers. "That should level the playing field a bit."

Chapter Eleven

Hank

HE KEPT HIS SMILE in place and looked around the bar, nodding at all the right spots. They were talking endlessly, going over the variables of what could go right and what could go wrong and all the while he could feel the dozen or so small wounds on his body fading, healing.

Meanwhile Joe said pretty words to calm Sam down. Apparently he wasn't the only one that didn't want people looking inside his head. The difference was, he could feel it when Joe started looking inside his skull, and it seemed like the rest of the group lacked that talent. He didn't know why he could, but it was something he intended to investigate.

He'd seen the losers in the van first, of course. He wasn't blind or deaf. Cody would have been lost, but that wasn't his fault. Cody was weaker physically and he was shy. Hank didn't have those problems. Hank was, well, Hank was pretty damned cool.

Not-Tina—who was staring daggers at Not-Kyrie in his lap when she wasn't drooling over Joe and Sam alike—asked what they'd do if they ran across the cops anywhere along the way. The question was interesting enough to get his full attention.

Joe shook his head. "No one wants cops here. Not us, not them, but it's always a possibility. The police show up, we run. They don't know who we are and we don't have ID for all of you yet. We could get out of the cells, I guess, but what if you change? What if you become Tina again? Last I checked, she had a few people who wanted her dead or alive."

"I can cover them." She waved a dismissive hand.

Joe got that stern look on his face again, as if he were here to parent all of them. "No, you can't. You think you can and maybe you could if it was just you." He held up a hand to stop her from protesting and Not-Tina's open mouth closed slowly, her objection held in check for the moment. "But you have Tina to consider. She's not you and she's not as strong as you. She breathes fire just fine, but there's no way she could hold her own against a bunch of goodfellas with a serious need to cut her down."

Not-Tina nodded.

"And by the way, have you figured out what we should call you yet? Not-Tina is hardly the best name." Joe raised an eyebrow and smiled as he spoke.

Not-Tina shot him a one-finger salute. "I'm gonna come up with a name, it's gonna take more than ten minutes, loser. I have to think about it."

"Don't think too hard. The longer you take, the longer we all have to wait to get you set up with papers."

Not-Tina bristled, putting her hands on the table, ready to stand up and start swinging.

Joe blinked and Hank smiled. Bronx thought he was charming enough to be a dick all the time, but he wasn't. What he was at the moment was in serious danger of having Not-Tina take a swing at him, and none of them needed to be beating on each other.

Sam looked to Not-Kyrie in Hank's lap—which, for the record, Hank was not complaining about at all—and said what was likely already on Not-Tina's mind. "She doesn't have a name yet either."

Not-Kyrie looked at Sam like he was aching to get his ass kicked. "It's none of your business what I have."

Joe looked at Sam and then at Not-Kyrie and opened his mouth, and Hank reached for the mostly empty beer pitcher on the table.

"What did you say to me?" Not-Tina was snarling.

"Hold on now, I didn't say a damned thing to you." Not-Kyrie's voice was just under a growl and he could feel her body tensing as she got ready to defend herself. She was looking at Sam, and Hank had no doubt that she was perfectly willing to clobber him for bringing her into the argument and killing her buzz.

Cody wasn't there. He was wherever he went when Hank was in charge, but Hank knew it was Cody's experiences that were painting his decisions. Cody was good at making distractions and cracking wise to defuse the situation. Cody would have probably made a few comments about how stupid he was and hammed it up to make sure that the angry people looked at him instead of at each other.

He wasn't Cody. He didn't play like that.

Cody wanted peace and quiet, and what Hank wanted was to have some fun. He looked at the bikers who'd been hogging the bar for the last hour or so and from time to time eyeing the girls at their table, and he hurled the beer pitcher at them as hard as he could.

"Heads-up!" His voice cut across the entire room and every last one of the bikers looked toward him, including the fat, bearded slob who managed to catch the pitcher with his face. The thing was plastic. If it had been glass, it would have probably knocked the biker into next week. Instead all that happened was he got a beer bath and let out a strangled, sputtered profanity as he headed for their table.

"You lost your mind? Just needed to get your stupid ass kicked?"

Hank was still grinning as he pulled Not-Kyrie off his lap, holding her as easily as an adult holds a baby. She let out a startled yelp and even through the shock, Hank could see the smile starting on her face. She wanted it too, the adrenaline and the noise and the fight.

Hank's foot caught the bottom of the table and he pushed it in the general direction of the approaching biker. Before the table could fall completely over, he kicked it the same as Cody would have kicked a soccer ball and sent it flying at Beer Boy.

"Bite me, loser!"

The table crashed into the beer-splattered biker and both of them went backward, skidding and staggering back into the rest of the Road Kings.

Joe looked at him as if he'd lost his mind. Joe didn't get it. He was used to this, all of this. He had his goals and he knew what he wanted from the world. Hank and the others, they were still new. While Joe wanted to plot his next move for getting rid of Hunter, Hank wanted to experience everything.

He rolled his shoulders and stretched his neck.

"Bring it, bitches!" He roared the words and started toward the bikers.

The Road Kings were hard men. On a national level, the motorcycle club dealt arms, sold drugs, probably had its hand in prostitution, and had a reputation for violence that had marked its members as trouble in almost every state in the continental US.

They didn't seem at all impressed by Hank despite his formidable size. The one closest to the bar charged right back at Hank, a battle cry starting on his lips.

Not-Kyrie grabbed the guy before he could reach Hank and spun him in a half circle before she smashed him back into the bar. Hank caught the next one at the same moment, his hand wrapping into the guy's face like a jock catching a basketball.

After that Hank didn't pay attention to the details, he just started swinging. He needed this. They all did.

They took out the Road Kings or they took out each other.

Joe was just too slow to notice that.

Chapter Twelve

Tina Carlotti

SHE OPENED HER EYES and immediately squinted against the glare of sunlight sneaking into the room from the dingy hotel window.

"Ow." Tina rolled over in the bed and almost smashed into Gene Rothstein's snoring face.

That took care of waking her up. Her heart pounded so hard she thought it might break out of her chest and run away. Yeah, okay, so Gene was cute and all, but she didn't need to keep waking up in bed with guys she barely knew or she was going to get a complex.

Gene continued snoring, oblivious to her dilemma. A quick check convinced her that she was still clothed. That helped. She didn't even like to think about her other self. So far her Other had robbed the neighborhood branch of the Mafia of a couple million dollars and gotten her in deep trouble with Tony Parmiatto and his boss, Paulo Scarabelli—and that was not going to be easily forgiven. She'd possibly brought about her mother's death—there would be no forgiveness for that—and she had guaranteed that no part of Tina's life was safe from getting screwed up beyond any hope of repair. And that was just in a few days, really. So she wasn't going to be too surprised if the bitch managed to get her into bed with a guy she barely knew. Gene could be as shy and cute as he wanted, but she wasn't exactly looking to hook up with anyone.

She looked around the room. Cody was sleeping on the cheap desk in front of the equally cheap hotel room mirror. He was small enough to get up there without trouble, but if Hank had been the one climbing up there, she was surprised that the desk hadn't collapsed under the weight of him. Cody was stripped down to his tighty whities, and he was apparently having a pretty good dream because while he was sleeping, parts of him were definitely awake. She didn't want to think of him that way, but there it was, loud and proud.

She turned away and saw that the other twin bed in the room was occupied by Hunter and Kyrie. She felt another twinge of jealousy flare through her. Kyrie was smoking hot, that was all there was to it. Every one of the guys had been trying to stare through her clothes since they'd met her. So far they hadn't much bothered with Tina, and while she wasn't actually looking for any romance—her life was crazy enough, thanks—it would have been nice to at least have them look now and then. Kyrie could wear a cardboard box and they'd check out her butt.

Tina carefully extracted her leg from between Gene's. He was clothed too, thank God. Unlike Cody, he was actually wearing his jeans. Once she'd untangled, Tina crawled out of the bed as quietly as possible and headed for the bathroom.

Her reflection in the mirror looked wrong. A flash of color that shouldn't have been there. Tina stopped and looked carefully, absolutely unaware of the shriek that started in her belly and boiled out past her lips like steam from a teakettle.

She was too busy looking at the long, serpentine shape that twisted around her arm. It slithered from her shoulder and wrapped itself around her bicep, her elbow and her forearm, ending at the striking snake head tattooed onto her wrist.

"Ohmigod!!!" She staggered back into the main room and sat on the bed, face level with Cody's belly button. Cody woke up with a sputtering moan, his eyes flying wide as he looked toward her. She looked at her own face, reflected on the other side of him, and screamed a second time. Cody tried to roll away from her screaming and instead bumped into the cold mirror. Half a second later he fell off the desk, his eyes wide and panicked.

Gene and Hunter and Kyrie all sat up, startled out of their unconscious states by her screams.

"What the hell did she do to me?" Tina's voice shook with fury as she looked at the snake tattoo, studying the details. "What the hell did she do?"

"What? What did who do?" Hunter was right next to her, his eyes projecting concern. She knew he wanted to protect her, but he couldn't. It was too late for that.

"That other me! She tattooed me!" Tina blinked hard to stop the tears that were threatening her. Not a chance she'd let any of them see her cry, not now, not ever.

Gene covered his mouth and looked away and in that moment she hated him. He was laughing at her! Oh, he was trying to hide it, but he was laughing just the same. She looked away from his smug, rich boy face before she could lose her temper.

Hunter stared hard, shocked, as if the idea that one of the Others could do such a thing never crossed his mind. That was crazy, he'd been dealing with Joe for a long time, and yet there he was, freaking out.

Kyrie moved closer to Tina and took her hand. She wasn't mocking or cruel or anything but kind, and Tina hated herself a little for her earlier jealousy and for the fact that part of her still wanted to be angry. Kyrie was nice. Kyrie was everything that a nice person was supposed to be, and that wasn't something Tina was used to in her world.

Kyrie's voice was no nonsense. "Come on. Let's see if we can't fix it."

"How can we fix this? It's a tattoo! It's permanent!"

"Maybe not. I heard you can wash them out if they haven't healed all the way. We just need to scrub your arm."

Even as she spoke, Kyrie gently pulled Tina toward the bathroom.

Tina caught a glimpse of Cody as he watched them go past. His face set with an expression she'd never seen on him before. She didn't know him well enough to figure out what it meant.

Tattoos are created by forcing colored inks under the skin and deep enough into flesh that the colors are effectively permanent. In order to get the colors down that deep, needles are required. In most people, the tiny holes caused by the ink are irritated and tender for a long while. But Tina's skin was already back to its usual level of sensitivity.

Not-Tina was different from Tina. She healed much faster. Despite Kyrie's very vigorous attempts at scrubbing the colors away, it was too late. The ink was permanent.

For just a moment, Tina thought about crying. She knew that Kyrie would be there to comfort her in an instant.

Instead she swallowed the tears and held on to the anger, letting it grow inside her. Tears were weakness. Anger was a weapon. Long as she remembered that, she'd be fine.

She told herself that until she believed it.

Chapter Thirteen

Hunter Harrison

HUNTER AND CODY LOOKED at the motorcycles outside their room with mutual expressions of shock. Not just motorcycles, but custom jobs. The sort of bikes that cost enough for a small house. Had anyone asked Cody what he knew of bikes he would have eagerly admitted that he knew nothing, but he knew enough to understand that the motorcycles in front of them—including the one he'd found the keys for in his pocket—were not the sort of thing someone would willingly let them walk away with.

"What happened?" Hunter asked the question to himself, but Cody shook his head in response.

"I think we're in it deep."

Hunter shot him a look. "Seriously? You think?" Cody shot him a look that said sarcasm wasn't really appreciated right then, and Hunter tried to reel his attitude back.

"I'm getting a few memories from this, dude. They aren't happy stuff. I think we took out a gang. And I think we took out the sort of gang that has a lot more members." His voice shook and he took two steps back. "I mean it. We're dead if they catch us with these bikes, man. Dead." He ran his finger along the name painted on the gas tank of one of the bikes. The Road Kings. "Seriously dead, and maybe maimed real bad before they get to the killing part."

Hunter shook his head. "Is this ever gonna stop?"

"Isn't that why we're here?" Cody moved around the parked motorcycles, taking in the details of each vehicle and shaking his head. "Isn't that why we're doing all of this? So we can make it stop?"

Hunter thought about that for a moment and finally nodded. "Yeah. But it'd be a lot easier if this sort of thing wasn't going on."

Cody shook his head And a small, puzzled grin played at his face. "Dude, I know how to ride a motorcycle. How did that happen?"

Hunter shrugged. "I guess Joe must have taught you last night."

"He can ride a bike?"

"Yeah, so can I. And I guess he must have taught me too. That stuff he said about us doing stuff that the Others learn, I guess it must go both ways."

Cody got a deeply worried look for a moment and then seemed to shrug it off.

"What's wrong?" Hunter needed them, all of them, to help him through this. While he wanted little more than to sit back and relax for a while—a chance to relax seemed impossible to find—he couldn't risk Cody or any of them having a meltdown.

"What's wrong?" Cody's voice rose in volume and octave as he answered. "Dude, I've got King Kong hiding inside me and I apparently just stole a bike from a motorcycle gang. I can't go home, I can't even talk to my parents, I've got all sorts of memories that aren't mine cramming into my head. Seriously, what *isn't* wrong?"

Hunter understood what he was feeling. He'd been feeling it for as long as he could remember. "Just calm down. Freaking out won't help."

"I think I have a reason for going a little crazy here, okay?" Cody waved his arms frantically. "Didn't exactly start my week with this crap in mind."

Hunter moved closer and put a hand on his shoulder, speaking softly so Cody would have to listen. "You make too much noise and we're going to get the wrong attention. Cops might not kill us, but they're going to make it really, really hard to get this done."

Cody stopped pacing and nodded. "We need to get out of here. I don't care if we're walking or taking these bikes, but we need to be gone—and soon."

"I agree." Hunter squinted and looked around. "I just wish I knew where they'd left car, because we might not have any way to take care of business if the money and weapons are gone."

Cody let out a groan and sat down on the sidewalk. "What the hell were they thinking?"

"Who?"

"Our other selves . . ."

"Look, let's just get back with the others and see if they know anything we don't."

Cody stared hard at him for several seconds before he finally stood back up and shook his head. "Hope one of them knows how to dodge bullets."

Back inside the hotel room things were little calmer. Poor Tina was still staring at her arm, trying to understand how she could have a permanent mark on her body without any recollection of how it got there.

Gene looked toward them as they entered the room. He was in the process of putting on his shoes. "We need food. Then we need to discuss what we're doing next." Kyrie nodded her agreement from where she sat next to Tina.

"The car is gone. We've got five motorcycles outside instead."

Gene nodded. "I already found the money and the weapons," Gene said. "They were stowed in the closet and under the bed." He pointed toward the door they'd just entered with his chin. "I told the maid we didn't need the room cleaned. Would have been hard to explain."

"So where are you going for food?"

Gene looked at Cody for a long moment. "I was thinking a restaurant would be good."

"Well, yeah, but where are there restaurants? We're in the middle of nowhere." Which was true enough. The hotel they were staying in was along the interstate and didn't seem to have much by way of choices unless you counted the liquor store across the eight lanes of traffic.

"Got a bike. I'll figure it out."

"You can't go alone." Hunter blurted the words out before he knew he was going to talk. He pressed his lips together, wishing he had a better edit button.

"I wasn't planning on it." He jerked his chin toward the girls. "Kyrie's coming along."

"What?" For an instant there was an unexpected flare of jealousy that rose from his stomach. He did his best to crush that sensation.

Gene got an irritated look on his face. "I need someone to get my back and you and Cody were busy. So Kyrie volunteered." That desire to take charge came back to Hunter along with the annoyance that Kyrie was leaving, but before he could make a comment, Gene spoke again. "We need food. Deal with it. When we get back, we can discuss what else we need to get done."

Without another word Gene moved toward the door, and despite an irrational desire to step between the boy and the door, Hunter let him get where he was going.

Kyrie shot a dark look in his direction as she brushed past and Cody chuckled.

"What?" He waited until the door was closed behind the couple heading for food before he asked Cody what was on his mind.

"Just thinking you better make sure Kyrie's your girl before you start acting all possessive about her." Cody's smirk was deeply annoying.

"What are you talking about?" Did he sound defensive? He didn't think so.

Apparently Tina disagreed. "He ain't wrong. I thought you were gonna start flexing your muscles and beating your chest when Gene said Kyrie was going along with him." As always, her tone left little room for disagreeing.

"But I wasn't. I didn't . . ." He didn't know how to finish the sentence.

Tina waved her hand dismissively. "Don't have to defend yourself to me. I don't really care."

He looked to Cody for backup, but he was wasting his time. Cody shook his head and that smarmy little smirk on his face only grew more pronounced.

"Whatever." He felt himself blush though he wasn't quite

sure why. Or if he was sure, he didn't want to admit it, not even to himself.

It took almost an hour for the two to get back with food, and during that time Hunter had to suppress the jealousy he refused to acknowledge on a dozen different occasions—a jealousy that he hadn't even been aware of until that morning. He kept peering out the windows and pacing, telling himself he was merely worried about them getting apprehended, which was partially true.

It was Tina who responded first when they came through the door, her voice a harsh crack. "Beginning to think you two had eloped or something. How far away from restaurants are we?"

Gene blinked, surprised by the attitude from Tina. Kyrie carried in bags of Chinese takeout and shook her head. "We had to wait for the restaurant to open. It was this or the diner we found next to Royal Gardens, and the diner looked like maybe it was closed."

"Closed?"

She frowned. Even unhappy, she looked cute. "It wasn't actually closed, but the parking lot was empty. Never eat at a diner that doesn't have a few cars in the parking lot."

"So what did you get?" Cody stared hungrily at the bags. He was a scrawny thing, but always hungry. Even as Hunter thought that, his stomach let out an audible growl. The scent of the Chinese food had awakened the hunger inside of him. Changing shapes—becoming Joe Bronx—took a lot of energy. The only way to replace the calories burned was to take in more calories.

Gene shrugged. "Five house-fried rice boxes and a five-person family sampler." Hunter looked around the room and realized they were all hungry, close to ravenous. The change affected them all the same way.

Kyrie swung a particularly ponderous bag onto the bed and it sloshed. "Got some sodas too."

For the next fifteen minutes, the conversations were kept to a minimum. Everyone was too busy shoving food down their throats to talk. Cody hammed it up on how good everything was and got everyone laughing—which, really, seemed to be his specialty. Hunter liked the skinny kid. He wasn't so sure about the monster hiding inside of him, but he definitely liked Cody. They ate. They ate to the point where they should have been groaning in pain because the portions were huge, but instead of being in pain they were merely sated.

They should have been on the move, Hunter knew that, but he needed time to think. Everything that had happened in the last few days had been so frantic and fast that he needed time to think. All he had to do was look at the others, and he knew they felt the same way. Still, there was that old saying about the elephant in the room and how everyone tries to ignore it, and he could also see that though no one was looking right at the problem, they all wanted to talk about it just the same.

So when they finished eating, he finally put it on the table. "We were attacked yesterday. I'm still a little fuzzy on the details."

Cody stuck his hand up in the air and started speaking immediately. "Bunch of goons attacked. Then they became bigger, badder goons. We got attacked by Successes."

"'Successes?'"

"Yeah, you know. If we're the Failures, they were the Successes."

Gene frowned. "I'm not a failure. I can't speak for the rest of you, but I'm not a failure." His tone was petulant.

Cody shook his head. "According to Joe Bronx is all I'm saying. And either way, dude, I'm a big fat zero, so you can feel just as special as you want to."

Gene started to say something, but Tina cut him off. "Hey! Let's just find out what Hunter has in mind and we can all get bitchy later. Right now, I want answers." She glared blue-murder at both of them as she snapped her words in their direction. And just that quickly, they reined in their emotions.

Hunter cleared his throat. "Thing is, we know we're being hunted by these other 'Successes.' To make matters worse, if Cody's right, we just pissed off a serious group of heavyweight hard asses called the Road Kings by stealing their bikes, at the very least."

Cody almost opened his mouth to say something else, but instead he only shrugged.

"So I have to think we were set up. I'm having serious doubts about this address in my pocket, and I think we need to check it out. Not all of us, just a couple. I think we need to know if we're in for another confrontation or if we have a chance of meeting this Evelyn Hope lady."

The TV had been playing in the background throughout their meal, and Kyrie's eyes widened as she looked at the screen. "Guys! Guys! Look!" She pointed and nearly jumped up and down as she reached for the remote with her free hand, increasing the volume.

Hunter looked, and as he did, he felt his stomach fall away, as if he were on the top of the highest peak on a roller coaster and was suddenly dropping, heading down the steep hill at nearly impossible speeds and leaving his stomach somewhere behind him.

Gene stared at the screen and Hunter saw the color drain from the other boy's face.

On the screen were three pictures of Gene, all of them relatively recent. He smiled nervously in all three images.

And the announcer on the TV spoke in calm, precise tones. He looked like a retired model who'd found a second career. "Once again, the young man in these images, Eugene Alexander Rothstein, has been missing for the last three days from his home in upstate New York. It is uncertain if he has been abducted or if he has left home voluntarily, but his parents have offered a substantial reward for information leading to his safe return." The man looked at the papers on the desk in front of him and the image changed to a shot of two people Hunter had never seen before. Gene had seen them. He flinched.

The man was dark haired and athletic though getting up enough in years that it was obvious his biggest days as a jock were in the past. The woman had long dark hair and dark brown eyes and she was pretty, but her features were sharp and harsh. He couldn't easily imagine her smiling. The names of the couple were printed at the bottom of the screen, but aside from the last name of Rothstein he'd forgotten them as soon as he looked.

It was Gene's mother that did the talking, reading off an index card, "Our son Eugene is missing, and we don't know for sure if he was abducted or forced to leave or if he left of his own volition—but whatever the case, we want our son back. To that end, we are offering one hundred thousand dollars for his safe return." A toll-free number scrolled across the bottom of the screen. Even though it was obvious that the woman had more to say, the screen cut back to the anchorman, who was smiling toothily for the camera.

The pictures shown previously popped up on the screen

again. "One hundred thousand dollars for information leading to the safe return of Eugene Rothstein to his family. We here at Channel Seven hope that one of our viewers might recognize the young man and be able to help reunite him with his family."

Gene reached for the remote, turned the TV off, stood up and started pacing in tight circles. His face was almost expressionless.

"Gene? What the hell?" That was Tina, who always seemed determined to get straight to the heart of the problem.

"My parents. We're screwed."

"Don't you think you're being a bit dramatic? All of our parents are probably on the news and trying to find us." Kyrie was moving even as she spoke. Probably moving to try to keep him calm, because his face was serene but his body language said he was ready to explode.

Gene shook his head and stared hard at her. "Not all of the parents out there are offering a hundred grand as a reward. No. You don't get it. She's not going to stop until she has me back at home. There's no halfway with her. She's like the Terminator, only meaner."

Silence reigned for several seconds. While everyone absorbed the information, Cody rubbed his hands over his arms and shivered. "Is it cold in here?"

Gene didn't even look at him as he responded. "No.

That's just my mom."

Despite himself, Hunter laughed. A moment later the others joined in. They were in deep, and sometimes the only way to survive the craziness was to laugh about it.

Chapter Fourteen

Evelyn Hope

MOST EVERYONE WHO KNEW Evelyn Hope was intimidated by her. She was a hard woman who disliked being kept waiting.

There was one exception, a man who was her equal in power and had known her since she was in high school. He understood her, knew exactly how her mind worked and had founded Janus with her.

Josh Warburton smiled tightly as she climbed from the corporate jet. He could have merely had a driver waiting to pick her up, but he preferred to see his old friend in person.

Warburton was a short man, all of five feet, seven inches in height; he was also portly, with a thick waist and a round face. His smile was easygoing and his fair skin was covered with a smattering of freckles. His dark green eyes and his light auburn hair led many people to think he looked a little bit like a leprechaun. No one in their right mind ever said as much to his face. Not even Evelyn, who could have probably gotten away with it.

The two of them smiled as they hugged. "Good to see you in person for once, Josh."

"It's been too long." She sighed as she held the man. They had been through so much together. When it came to business on the phone, they were cordial. Business was business and always came first, but on those rare occasions when they got together, she could look at the man who was practically family and she could let herself relax just a bit. It was a wonderful feeling that she seldom experienced.

"So." Josh looked away from her and broke the embrace. "Subject Seven? Really, Evelyn?"

"No one was more surprised than me, Josh. I thought he'd fallen off the face of the earth." She looked away from him, forcing back the emotions that threatened to surface. She could not think of Seven without thinking about Tom and Bobby, the husband and the son lost to the monster she'd helped create.

"We'll find him, Evvy. We'll find him and we'll capture him." His voice was soft, kind. He knew everything, of course, understood every aspect of what she was going through, because he was the one who'd helped make everything possible. She and Tom had been the brains behind the work. Josh had been the one who took care of the money, the legalities and the everyday events. Josh was a genius when it came to money and paperwork, just as surely as she was a genius when it came to genetics. He had also learned enough from her that he could keep up with her on the discussions of the processes they used, even if he couldn't exactly work out all of the details.

"Have you heard anything about them since the attack?" Josh's question drew Evelyn out of her small reverie.

She arched an eyebrow and allowed another smile. "You mean aside from the massive reward offered for bringing one of them back to his parents?"

Josh grinned. "I thought you might have heard about that."

Evelyn waved a dismissive hand. "Please. As if anything of that nature would escape George." Even as she spoke, she could see her assistant slowly climbing from the private jet, already engaged in conversation with God knew who.

Josh looked at the man and nodded. George, despite being in the middle of a heated debate on his cell phone, immediately nodded and waved a greeting.

"He's a bit of a lifesaver, isn't he?" Josh knew the score. He understood exactly how much Evelyn depended on George. He also knew that she would drop her assistant off a cliff in a heartbeat if it meant furthering her goals in life. She did not allow herself the luxury of love, with very few exceptions.

"Tell him that and I'll kill you myself, but yes." She

smiled and stepped past him. "What do we know about Eugene Rothstein?"

"He's the right age. His paperwork is in perfect order. He could have been adopted from any number of legitimate agencies." Josh shook his head. "The good news is I recognized the signatures on the paperwork. Hanson and Clarkson."

The two men who had started all of this madness by selling the kids in an adoption scam. Now, instead of relaxing, Evelyn and Josh were trying to clean up a mess started by a couple of dissatisfied ex-employees who had already been taken care of apparently, since they could not be found.

"What about his family?"

"Old money and lots of it. The offer is legitimate." Josh's face was calm; his eyes were lit up with excitement. He had information and there was little he loved more than sharing his secrets with Evelyn. "The thing is, he's not the only one. We have to figure out who the rest of them are."

"Well, yes, that would be one of the reasons I called you, Josh. You were the one who tried to warn me before."

He almost said I told you so. She could see that he wanted to, but he was wise enough to keep it to himself. "I've got a list. Twenty names all told. We just need to figure out which names were contacted by Subject Seven." Twenty names? The thought was unsettling. She'd hoped for no more than four or five. Twenty of the monsters out there? All of them as unpredictable as Subject Seven? It was enough to make her palms sweat.

"Well, I think we can safely assume one of them is the Rothstein boy."

"I've already got people working on finding the rest of them and establishing surveillance. As soon as we know who's with him, we can round up the rest of them and get everything back to normal."

Evelyn looked at George as he hung up the phone. "How did it go?"

George looked at her and nodded, not saying a word. He didn't need to. She understood his simple gesture. That was another of the reasons she kept him around.

Josh did not understand what his nod meant and looked like he wanted desperately to ask. Evelyn smiled. Let him keep guessing. She'd tell him when everything was set up. Until then, she felt like keeping a few secrets to herself.

Chapter Fifteen

Cody Laurel

"HI, MOM." CODY'S HEART hammered in his chest as he heard his mother's voice. Maybe she wasn't his biological mom, but he didn't care about that. Oh sure, it was going to be an issue at some point in the future, and it was already on his mind a good deal, but the simple pleasure of hearing her voice eliminated his worries about everything else. She was his mom. That was enough. He missed her. Worse than that, he felt like he was coming down with something, and that only made him feel more homesick. His mom made the best chicken soup in the universe and swore it could cure almost any illness. He believed it, too.

"Cody?" Oh, how her voice broke and shook and he hated knowing that he was the cause of her tears.

"Hi. Listen, I can't talk long. I just wanted to let you know that I'm okay. I'll be home as soon as I can, but there's stuff I have to do."

Lies. All lies. He wasn't okay. He felt like crap. His skin was clammy and he had a bad case of the shakes and he thought maybe he was going to puke his guts out if he looked at Chinese food ever again. Maybe it was food poisoning; but if so, he was the only one who had eaten anything bad.

"Cody, honey, you have to come home. Please. I need you here with me." Guilt twisted his guts into a new and even more unpleasant shape as he listened to her words. He'd never wanted to leave home—never wanted any of what was happening—but having his Other hanging around was like carrying a loaded gun in each hand and then juggling. Sooner or later one of the damned things would go off and someone would get hurt. He wasn't as worried about himself—well, okay, that was a consideration but not a big one—as he was about Hank hurting his mom or his dad. The male parental unit liked to yell, and Hank liked to kill things that annoyed him, so, yeah, best to keep the two well away from each other.

"Mom. It's for you and Dad, okay? There's some serious stuff going on and I don't want to take any chances on you guys getting hurt."

"Cody, we can take care of ourselves. We can take care of you. If there's a-a problem with the police, we can get you a lawyer." So much desperation in each word that came from her mouth and he could see her in his mind, her wide eyes starting to water, her lips trembling, and the very thought made his stomach twist again because she was one of the best people he'd ever known.

"Mom. I love you. Just remember that. I'll be home soon." He killed the call before she could hear him cry. God, he missed his parents.

Tina took the phone from him and gave him a quick hug. He didn't expect it and had no idea how to react, but he took the comfort she offered just the same.

Chapter Sixteen

Kyrie Merriwether

KYRIE WATCHED GENE'S FACE work through a storm of emotions before he finally lowered his brows in frustration and almost threw the phone to Tina. The other girl caught the phone and walked it over to Kyrie.

After that, it was only a matter of getting up the courage to call her dad on his cell at work.

He was on another call, so she made it quick and left a message on his voice mail. "Hi, Dad. It's me. I'm okay. I think maybe I could be back as early as next week. I love you and Mom and everyone. Okay. Bye."

She gave the phone to Tina and moved away, hugging herself in the bright sunlight. The sun was doing its job, but the air still had a chilly edge. Or maybe it was just that she missed her family. She couldn't really say.

Tina opened the back of the phone and pulled the battery from it. A moment later the phone went in the trash can and the battery went into Tina's pocket. Kyrie understood the logic. Tina was afraid that they could be traced through the cell phone calls, and she was probably right about that. Still, despite everything, she thought maybe Tina was being paranoid. Not that she would have said that to Tina's face.

Tina didn't speak to any of them. Kyrie could see her struggling, fighting against whatever grief she was feeling. They'd known each other for less than three days—she thought it was three days; the sense of time she used to know no longer made sense—but all of them knew that Tina's father was long in his grave and that her mother had been killed and dumped in the river near her home, probably by the same mobsters that Tina's Other had robbed.

Tina was tiny, but she was also hard. She almost never let anyone see anything but what she wanted them to see. Kyrie didn't know if she envied the other girl that trait or felt sorry for her because she was so good at it. Kyrie herself had been raised in a very different world, with two parents and five brothers and sisters.

But they had things in common just the same. They were the two girls in a group of five, and they had Others.

Near as Kyrie could figure out (and she was thinking about it constantly), Joe Bronx had managed to wake up their Other selves. She wasn't completely sure about that, but she knew that he knew things he shouldn't about all of them, from the way he'd talked before. And she knew that her Other had come along and, at the very least, had stolen a truck full of weapons for Joe Bronx before she even knew that she had an Other.

Her Other scared the heck out of her. And that was one more reason to rub her arms in an effort to stay warm, thank you very much. She didn't remember much of anything about the change happening, but she knew that when her Other rose up to take over, she was always, always angry. She could feel the fury that boiled underneath the surface of the Other's mind, like a bad aftertaste. Her Other was hungry—not just for experiences, but for everything. She resented being forced down by Kyrie. She resented Kyrie's existence.

She looked over at Tina again, her eyes tracing the length of the snake tattoo on her arm. It was a beautiful piece of work. No two ways about it. Highly detailed. And that worried her a bit. Because while she didn't have any tattoos herself, she knew a few people who had them, and much smaller tattoos than the one on Tina's arm had taken hours to finish and sometimes several sessions.

Either Not-Tina had met up with an amazingly fast artist, or several people had worked on her arm at the same time, or they had been out for longer than one day. And that, well, that was definitely enough to make her skin feel cold. She had no way of knowing how long she'd been away from home anymore because everything was blurred in her mind.

Her memories didn't feel right: they felt fuzzy and distorted.

She pulled herself out of her musing as Hunter approached, his face as worried as ever. He was cute, but she didn't let herself dwell on that. There were lots of cute guys back home too. Luke and Dan and Erik came to mind, and she knew them better.

Still, she loved the way his face softened and almost relaxed when he looked at her. It made her feel good about herself. It was even a little flattering—and a lot annoying, thank you very much—the way he'd acted when she and Gene went to get food, but that was just another thing she didn't really want to contemplate too carefully.

Then he opened his mouth and ruined it.

"We have to go. We need to get to a store and buy some clothes, and then we have to scope out the address we have and see if it's a trap."

Gene looked back at him and frowned. "You're not going to like me for saying this, but we're not the best ones to do this."

"What other choices do we have?" Hunter shook his head. "We can't exactly go hiring a private detective, can we?"

Kyrie didn't like the look on Gene's face. She knew what he was going to say before he said it.

Tina beat him to the punch. "He means the Others. He wants you to let Joe Bronx out so he can maybe take a look around." As she spoke, she stared hard at Hunter. Her face was completely neutral—her eyes gave away nothing.

Cody coughed into his hand and looked away, his skin pasty. Kyrie saw that a thin layer of sweat was forming on his forehead. He looked like he was going to get sick any second.

Hunter opened his mouth to object, and Tina cut him off. "He's right, too. Joe's been doing this stuff for a long time, and him and the Hydes, whatever we might like or not like about them, they're better at this than we could ever be. So you need to let Joe out to do his thing."

"Hydes?" Gene interrupted, that puzzled look back on his face.

"It's a joke." Tina waved her hand dismissively. "We're Jekylls, they're Hydes. We behave"—she pointed at her arm—"and they get us in trouble."

Even as Tina was explaining the terminology, Hunter turned his eyes to Kyrie. "I don't know how."

Tina shrugged her narrow shoulders and beat Kyrie to the punch. "Just stop fighting him. Let him win."

Kyrie knew Tina was right. That was all that Hunter had to do: just give in to the thing that was hiding inside of him. And that, too, made her shiver.

Chapter Seventeen

Sam Hall

THEY WERE SLEEPING, THE whole lot of them, when Sam Hall opened his eyes and rolled carefully out of the bed. Hunter might have wanted to save money, but the females with him had won their fight for a separate room. Hunter slept on one bed and Cody slept on a rollaway bed near the closet. For just a moment, Sam thought about killing both of them, not because he had anything against them, but merely because he knew it would bother Gene to no end. Precious little Gene didn't like violence—or at least he told himself that he didn't like it.

Sam sniffed the air and looked toward Cody. The boy was soaked in sweat and shivering in the heated air of the hotel room. He was sick. He smelled like death, like something inside of him was falling apart and rotting and the rest of his body was working on catching up. Gene was stifled by narrow senses, but Sam did not suffer from the same flaws. He could see and hear and taste and smell so much more than his Other. If he'd had the time, he could have spent hours simply experiencing the differences between himself and the weak little boy that shared the same space with him.

And Gene *was* weak; there was simply no other way to put it. Gene was willing to listen to Joe Bronx and Hunter and accept their orders without question. Sam didn't much like that notion. What Sam didn't like, he fixed.

Perfect example: the Right Revrund Robbie—the preachy drunk who was the best friend of Gene's adoptive father and the first victim of Sam's anger when he hurt Gene's feelings by telling him he'd been adopted. The man thought he knew everything there was to know about how the world worked. Booze made him think he was something special. Gene always listened to the pompous bastard prattle on and just took it. Sam had taken matters into his own hands. He was just a little surprised to hear the loser had survived being thrown off a three-story balcony. That was okay. He could always fix that problem when he got back home.

Moving with stealth that would have surprised almost anyone, Sam slipped from the room and snuck down the hallway to the stairs leading to the main floor of the motel. It was a dive. No surprise there. His stomach grumbled, and he noticed that there was a restaurant nearby. He deviated from his plans long enough to grab two burgers and flirt with the waitress for a few minutes before heading to the pay phones in the parking lot of the motel.

Three phones. The first one was broken. The second one worked just fine. He dialed the numbers after a very brief struggle to extract them from his memory. Gene might have worried about how Sam could possibly know his home phone number, but Sam didn't care. He had what he needed, and that was all that mattered.

An unfamiliar voice answered the phone after the third ring. He was expecting the voice of one of Gene's parents. His plan was simple, really. He was going to offer to bring Gene back in exchange for the reward. It was a lie, of course, but by the time they figured that out, he'd have the money secreted away somewhere. He wasn't even sure of the details, but he knew he could figure them out given enough time. It would take at least a day to take a bike back from Chicago to New York.

All of that went away when he heard a stranger say hello.

"Who is this?"

"I was about to ask you the same question. It's a bit late to be calling a family at home, don't you think?"

He actually hadn't given it any thought. He didn't care if he woke the bitch before promising to bring back her little boy.

"Who are you?"

"My name is Evelyn Hope. And you? What name are you going by?"

That was a strange way to phrase the question, and it made the hairs on his neck stand on edge.

"You can call me Sam Hall."

"Hi, Sam. Why were you calling the Rothsteins so late at night?"

"I have a business proposition for them." He almost growled the words. He didn't like this woman. She sounded too confident, and he resented her for it.

"Sam, are you Gene's Doppelganger?"

"What? How could you know—?"

"Sam. I made you and your friends. There are certain tricks I've learned for understanding who I'm dealing with."

For the life of him he couldn't decide if she was bluffing.

"What do you want, then?"

"I'm sorry?" Hope's voice was taken aback. "What do you mean?"

"I mean I called Gene's parents. I got you. I bet his folks don't even know about you because if they did, they wouldn't want you anywhere near their precious little boy." Sam smiled. She'd gotten almost as shaken up as him, and that meant she wasn't anywhere near as confident as she was trying to sound.

"Well, I think we probably want the same things, Sam. Or at least we want things that can be mutually beneficial."

That little tremor was gone from her voice. He might have caught her off guard, but he had no doubt the woman he was dealing with was used to being in charge. He could respect that.

"Here's what I want. I want money. And I want you to leave me alone. I don't care about Gene. I don't care about any of them. I want money, and I want to get rid of Gene, and I most definitely don't want to get to know you better."

The woman's voice on the phone was soft, but she laughed. A short little sound that was followed by almost a minute of silence before she spoke again. "You're very direct, Sam Hall. I respect that."

He nodded. "Good. Then maybe we can come to a deal."

"Maybe we can, Sam." She paused again, a long silence that was filled with possibilities. "Maybe we can at that."

"What do you want, Evelyn? What do you want in exchange for giving me what I want?"

"I want to know when and where I can find all of you. I want to get Subject Seven back as quickly as I can and without anyone getting hurt."

That last part was a lie. He could almost sense it. She said it because she was supposed to say it. And who the hell was Subject Seven? Sam smiled to himself. There was only one possibility, really. There was only one in their group who said he'd been experimented on. Joe Bronx had to be Subject Seven.

"And in exchange, can you give me freedom? Freedom from you and freedom from Gene?"

"Freedom from Gene?"

"He bores me. I don't want him around."

"Is that what you want, Sam? Freedom from your other self?"

"Wouldn't you?" He made himself calm down. He was too close to the hotel to start screaming. "If you found out there were two minds inside your body, wouldn't you want to be free of the other one?"

She was silent for several moments, except for the sound of her breathing. They were already coming for her. Maybe she knew that and maybe she didn't, but he thought he could use it to his advantage. This was a chance to bargain with her, to get whet he needed for what she would have gotten anyway. Perfect. Absolutely sweet.

"I suppose I would at that, Sam. I'll tell you what. I get you along with the others when the time comes and I'll see what I can do to stop the changes from ever happening again."

"And I should trust you why, Evelyn?"

She sounded bored when she answered. "What other choice do you have, Sam? I'm the only person alive who could possibly fix your problem."

"We're supposed to look your place over tomorrow, see if it's a trap. Only a couple of us, though. Not all of us. You want all of us, you have to work with me here. When we get there, I'll either leave you a note near the door or I'll call you back tomorrow night around the same time, whichever is better to avoid getting noticed. In exchange, I get freedom and you get the rest of them without a fight. Or at least with less of a fight. You'll know when to look for us and whether or not we're armed."

"That sounds wonderful."

"Evelyn?"

"Yes, Sam?"

"You made us, right?"

"Yes."

"Then you know how strong we are. You know how serious I am when I say I'll kill you if you do me wrong."

"There's no reason to do you wrong, Sam. My goal has always been to get Seven back."

"Just making sure we understand each other."

He hung up the phone and moved back toward the hotel. That had gone better than he'd expected.

Chapter Eighteen

Tina Carlotti

TINA SAT UP IN the bed. The room was dark, but that didn't bother her. Easily one week out of three while she was growing up was without electricity. You had to pay the bills, or they cut off the power. Her mom had never been very good at paying the bills on time.

She tried to push the thoughts of her mother away, but it was late and she was tired and the memories crept past her defenses and kicked the crap out of her heart yet again. There was nothing she could do about it, so she pulled her knees in close to her chest and lowered her head until her face was hidden. Then she cried as quietly as she could. It was quiet enough to avoid waking up Kyrie, who was softly snoring on the other bed.

She wanted to sleep. She hadn't slept worth a spit in

two days, and before that she was too tired to really relax. Instead she just closed her eyes and woke up a few hours later. Tina was used to remembering her dreams, and now she didn't even seem to have any to remember. Maybe whenever she was asleep, her Other showed herself. That wasn't a comforting notion.

She looked toward the wall between her room and Hunter's and shook her head. He wasn't interested. She knew that. She could take one look at the boy and see that his eyes were damned near superglued to Kyrie. He had the hots for her roommate in a big way, and who could blame him? She was curvy in all the right spots, had a smile that could light up a room and never seemed to lose her temper about anything. Not even when Cody had fallen asleep in the car and used her as a pillow, complete with a trail of drool from his mouth that got all over her shirt. Girl was practically a saint. Tina would have made sure Cody woke his sorry-ass up, no questions.

Kyrie let out a soft sigh and rolled over on her side. Tina looked at the other girl for a long moment, appreciating the girl's beauty and simultaneously hating her for it.

It wasn't that Tina was ugly. She knew that. Her skin was clear, her eyes were nice, her dark curls were enviable. But next to Kyrie she might as well have been another guy.

Tina sighed and stood up, moving carefully to the window and looking out into the darkness.

And she saw Sam as he moved along the side of the road leading back to the interstate. He was a good distance away, but she recognized him from his photo. The way he moved, the way all of the Others moved, was different than the way most people moved. It was hard to define, really, except they seemed lighter on their feet and more fluid. And the way they listened, looked at the world around them; it was predatory. They didn't walk. They hunted. They didn't just look at other people: they assessed them, studied their strengths and weaknesses. Maybe it was something built into them or maybe it was just because they were new to the world, but they were different on an elemental level.

She thought about Hunter again and then about Joe Bronx. And then she looked at Sam as he walked down the road and compared him to Gene.

Sam was different. He maybe didn't like dirt, but he didn't dislike it either. He was willing to experience getting filthy just so he could say he'd rolled around in the mud. Tina could understand that. If she wasn't such a coward, she'd have been more like that herself. But she was afraid of a lot of stuff, even if she didn't like to let it show.

Her mom was dead. The only family she had left in the world was dead and gone, just that fast. The others had something to look forward to, to get back to. What did she have? A damned tattoo and a Hyde to her Jekyll, who wanted to be in charge. There weren't a lot of options open for her. She really didn't have much to win or lose from what was going on around her. The others all wanted something, all needed to get something from Evelyn Hope. There was nothing for Tina to get.

Mostly, right at the moment, she was afraid of how much she wanted to be someone special to Hunter. Oh, she understood it well enough. She wasn't stupid. Her only family was dead and she was on the run and Hunter gave off a sort of calm confidence that he wasn't even aware of. He was cute, yeah, but he was also strong. He had an edge, he was angry and he was driven. He knew what he wanted and he was the sort of guy that would get it, no matter how long it took.

Being around Hunter, well, it just made her feel like no matter what, things were going to be okay eventually. She wanted that security in her world because everything else was screwed up.

Outside of her window Sam turned around on the road and looked directly at her. She had no doubt that he'd seen her. She couldn't see the expression on his face from this distance or guess what he was thinking, but she doubted it was anything pleasant.

Not-Tina wouldn't have cared. Not-Tina might even have smiled. But Tina wasn't the same person as her Other. She had no idea why he was outside—why he was wandering around in the middle of the night—but Sam scared her. Not that she'd ever let him see that. No one got to see that. Not now, not ever.

And especially not Hunter. He was falling for Kyrie. He chose the pretty girl over her.

She hated him just a little bit for that. Even though her heart beat faster when he was around, even though she had trouble looking away from him, she hated him just that little tiny bit for liking the other girl instead.

And that scared the hell out of her.

Because even though she couldn't remember much of anything that Not-Tina did, she understood that her Other reacted to her moods. If she hated Hunter—or Kyrie for winning his affections so easily—it was possible that Not-Tina would hate him too.

And Not-Tina seemed to like destroying whatever she hated.

Chapter Nineteen

Cody Laurel

THE FEVER WAS GETTING worse. Cody felt like he was sitting on a gigantic ice cube. He couldn't stop shivering, and his teeth were chattering too.

The worst part was, he was asleep and he could still feel it, that damned cold sensation that refused to leave him alone. If he'd been able to muster up the strength—or if he'd even been conscious in any real sense of the word—he would have tried to get himself to the shower and soak in a blast of hot water, anything at all to make the cold go away.

On the other bed, he heard the sound of Hunter moaning in his sleep. The boy rolled toward him and his eyes opened, but they didn't see Cody. Didn't see anything. They were open, yes, but whatever he was seeing, it was strictly in his mind. He was still asleep and dreaming.

"Nnnoduddeeno." The words were gibberish, whimpered past sleep-numbed lips. Cody sat up, shocked into motion.

The cold was as bad as ever, but for a moment at least he was distracted from the discomfort.

He was looking into Hunter's sleeping eyes when the change took place. It was smooth and seemed almost easy. When he felt himself changing from Cody into Hank, there was a lot of pain, an overwhelming hammer of agony that ran through him, but Hunter grew, changed, warped into Joe Bronx without any indication of discomfort.

One moment he was looking into the sleep-filled eyes of Hunter Harrison. The next, Joe Bronx was looking back at him, taking his measure. The differences were unsettling and substantial. It wasn't just that Joe was bigger—a given, really—it was his whole demeanor the way a sudden cunning appeared in the eyes.

"You look like shit, Cody. No offense. How're you feeling?"

Cody sat up straighter, his heart slamming. The look in Bronx's eyes—the expression on his face—they were familiar to Cody. He'd seen them a million times on the faces of the bruisers who'd liked to pick on him. There was a dark joy in that look, a savage pleasure that came from knowing that the person in front of you was easy prey.

Deep inside of him, Hank responded. He could feel his Other stirring, wanting to be free.

Cody shook his head. "I'm good. Just that food from earlier, it didn't sit so well."

Joe slid off the bed, moving with that unsettling panther gait of his. He looked back at Cody as he headed for the bathroom. Monster or not, everyone had to pee now and then.

"Well, you'll get better soon. We always do. And what doesn't kill us makes us stronger."

"Who said that? Darwin?"

Bronx shook his head and stopped on his entry to the bathroom long enough to frown in concentration. "Friedrich Nietzsche, maybe. But he was thinking of me when he said it."

Cody sighed. No ego there, no sir.

Around the same time the toilet was flushing, Not-Gene came into the room, looking momentarily surprised to see Cody awake and Joe off his bed. He recovered quickly.

"Feeling any better?" Cody was surprised to hear anything like concern from the brute standing in front of him. One look at the other's face told him the question was only a formality. He really didn't care.

"Sam. I was wondering where you were." Joe stepped into the room, his eyes locking on the other Doppelganger. Cody frowned. Sam? He guessed Not-Gene had finally picked a name. Whenever that had happened, he must not have been paying attention.

Sam shrugged. "Got hungry."

"Expect a lot of that. The more you change, the hungrier you get."

The bruiser held up a bag. "I brought coffee."

"You have to love late-night diners, don't you? Two in the morning and you can still get fresh coffee. Good man." Joe smiled as he reached for the bag.

"So what are we up to?"

Joe patted his pocket. "Got a little note from Hunter. They figure maybe it's best if a couple of us look over the address we were given. Check to see if it's a legitimate spot or a trap."

Sam snorted. "It's a trap. Of course it's a trap."

Cody interrupted. "Or, maybe, it's where the Evelyn woman lives. Or an office where we can visit her. Not gonna know for sure until we check. That's all." He stopped talking as the two stared at him. He hadn't been thinking or he would have stayed off their radar.

Joe looked Sam over with no real expression on his face. Cody knew that look too. He was taking Sam's measure and deciding if he was an equal or prey. Predators did that sort of thing. At least the human ones did. As the number-one victim at his high school, Cody knew the way the bullies thought. He had to if he wanted to survive. "Probably it is a trap. But we still have to check."

Sam nodded. "So let's get this done."

Joe looked into Cody's eyes. "You gonna be okay on your own?"

"Yeah." He felt a flash of resentment. He wasn't a baby.

They were all the same age. The fact that he was almost as small as Tina made the apes in the room feel like they were better than him.

Joe smiled, a look that was pure venom. "We'll be back soon." Cody looked back and felt that flash of anger again. Joe was asking about him solely because he knew it would offend. That was the way he liked to get his kicks. Cody would have bet money on it.

The other two left the room and he watched them leave. He wanted to resent Joe, but then again, the cold of the room was impossible to ignore. He slipped back under the covers on the rollaway bed and shivered. The fever was the worst he could remember ever having.

He told himself that the food poisoning was the only reason he had to shiver. Better not to admit how much the Others scared him—or how much it hurt him to change. Can't show weakness to predators. If you do, they tend to want to pounce.

Chapter Twenty

Kyrie Merriwether

TINA AND KYRIE WERE up and looking out the window when Joe and Sam left the hotel room. Sleep was proving elusive for Tina, and Kyrie had awakened when she heard the sounds of conversation from the next room. Tina didn't seem to have heard anything. Kyrie told herself it was only because the other girl was lost in thought. She didn't like to think about the way her senses were changing, becoming more acute. If she didn't think about the way she was changing—or the fact that her Other was becoming more dominant—it didn't worry her.

Kyrie sat up in her bed, then moved to the window and looked out at the two Others as they left the next room. They moved with the grace of predators, which was a strange thing to see firsthand. Each of them was large, six feet tall and then some. But despite the fact that they were on the third floor of the hotel and the way the cheaply built walkway had creaked as they moved up into the rooms earlier, the two large men didn't cause the walkway to so much as whisper a protest.

Kyrie rubbed her arms for warmth though she felt no real chill. Cody would have understood—though he probably would have denied it.

Tina moved away from the window. The show was over. She went back to studying the tattoo on her arm, her face darkening with anger as she examined the elaborate details.

"How long you think we were gone this time?" Her words were fast, clipped and demanding. She was angry.

"What do you mean?"

Tina held her arm up and rotated it so that Kyrie could see as much of the tattoo as possible. "This took hours. Maybe even days. How long do you think our Hydes were in charge before we came back?"

And just like that the chill was worse. Kyrie shook her head.

"I don't think I want to know."

"I do." Tina put her arm down. "I want to know. I want every one of those hours back."

"Well, I don't think you're going to get them."

Tina looked her in the eyes, dead on, with a darkness in her expression that was as intimidating as the monsters that had just left the other room. "Watch me. I'll get 'em. If I don't, I'm gonna take it out of Joe's hide."

"Why Joe?"

"Because he did this to us!" Tina's voice was a whip crack in the still air of the room. "He woke them up so they could help him! I don't care what he wants, what he needs, I can't stand this anymore!" She stood up and waved her arms around, frustrated. "I'm afraid to go to sleep! What if I wake up and it's been two months? What if the stupid bitch gets me arrested or knocked up? What then?"

And there it was, the fear masked by anger. Kyrie could understand that one. She'd woken up in different states, with blood on her hands on the way to waking up in Boston. Blood, and probably not her own. Kyrie was trying not to think about it, but apparently it was something Tina couldn't avoid. The girl next to her had gone to sleep and woke with her mother dead and the mob wanting to talk to her about a lot of money. Then she woke up with a serious ink job on her arm and no way to get rid of it. Her Other was marking her territory and Tina had lost control somewhere along the way and that was it in a nutshell, that was what was scaring Kyrie, even when she didn't want to admit it to herself. If it was happening to Tina, what was to stop it from happening to her?

"I wish I could make it better, Tina." It was all she could say.

Tina looked at her for a moment and then returned to her bed without responding.

Ten minutes later Tina was asleep.

That was something at least. A little while later, she fell into a fitful sleep herself.

Chapter Twenty-One

Sam Hall

THEY LOOKED THE HOUSE over carefully from a decent range. There was no sign of activity, but Joe cautioned Sam with his mental voice, telling him not to expect the lack of motion to prove anything.

Sam listened, silently studying the two-story house. It was nothing special, just another house on a block of twelve houses that were almost interchangeable.

Start three houses down. Look over each place and see what's going on inside. Be careful. We don't want to be seen. Joe spoke through their connection and then moved, slipping through the shadows and reappearing halfway down the block, starting at the other end of the street. Sam didn't question him. Instead he looked at the houses and did as he'd been instructed, checking the yards and then moving in, peering through windows with open curtains, carefully studying the contents of each home that he examined. Each and every one of them had all the signs of a family. There was furniture, personal belongings, and, in one case, a few toys in the yard.

He felt the fine hairs on the back of his neck rise as he realized that every house he carefully examined was empty of people. His senses, so much sharper than his Other's, said there was nothing, no one breathing or sleeping or moving inside the buildings.

What the hell? It's after midnight. Where is everyone? He sent the question toward Joe as he watched the Alpha slip closer to him.

They're expecting us. They don't want witnesses. Either they own every house on the block or they made sure no one would be home for a few days. Either way, this is all a trap. We're being set up so they can knock us down.

Now I just have to let her know when and where. Sam would have to call Evelyn. There weren't enough distractions for him to try leaving a note. Joe might notice if he tried to leave something behind.

Joe moved fast, ducking down below the windows and vanishing into shadows with a skill that Sam could only envy. The Other was adept at not being seen. Despite senses that were so much more accurate than Gene's, Sam still had trouble tracking Bronx's progress.

And then Joe rose in front of him, spilling out of the darkness like a ghost suddenly materializing. When he spoke again, it was with his mouth. "We need to not be here. They haven't spotted us yet, and I want to keep it that way."

"Who's gonna spot us?"

Joe shook his head. "Cameras, security for the area, anyone who happens to drive by." His answer was tense. "There's three glass bubbles, one on top of each streetlight. Probably a camera inside each one. But if anyone's seen us, they haven't reported us yet. Or the responders haven't shown yet. Either way, let's go."

Sam nodded and did his best to keep up as Joe headed away from the street that had been set up to take them down.

Ten minutes later they stopped at a convenience store and grabbed a dozen candy bars.

When they were out of the store and heading for the hotel, Joe spoke again. "They're expecting us. We're not going to disappoint them. But I want to make sure that when we meet up with whatever they've got planned, it's under our control. I want to know what's coming."

"Why aren't we just leaving? We know it's a setup, so why are we hanging around?"

Bronx eyed him and shook his head. "Sam, whether or not we get to surprise Evelyn, she's still got all the answers we need. We're going to have to meet up with her. I just want to make sure that we have contingencies in place, okay? If they try to kill us this time, I want to have weapons so we can fight back. If they want us to surrender peacefully, well, that's not how I do things. We need to let them know that we are serious about what's going on, and that means we have to fall for their little trap. But we aren't really getting set up here; we're coming in on our terms."

"How are we going to keep control?" Sam looked at the creature that had given him life and suppressed a twinge of guilt. Guilt was for the weak, and he would not allow himself to be weak.

"Simple. Reconnaissance. We send the girls here tomorrow. Let them walk down the street and see what there is to see in the daylight. Then we follow their lead."

"Why the girls?"

Joe chuckled. "Because half the country is looking for Gene, they might know what Hunter looks like and Cody is puking his guts out."

Sam nodded. "What then?"

"Then we come back, follow them and take these bastards out. And then we find Evelyn Hope and get what we need from her once and for all." Joe's voice was direct. His eyes were looking toward something beyond Sam's vision.

That suited Sam just fine. As long as he didn't start looking too close to home. Being a traitor was the sort of work that made Sam feel a little nervous, and Joe was exactly the sort that could damned near smell fear.

Joe wanted answers. Gene wanted answers. Sam didn't

care about answers. He wanted solutions and his freedom. And everyone else? Well, as his namesake liked to say, Damn your eyes.

One phone call, just a quick one to let Evelyn know that they were coming, that there would be an advance party and that weapons would be involved. That would be enough to keep his end of the deal with the woman.

Instant freedom.

He split off from Joe when they reached the hotel. Bronx stared at him, an unspoken question on his lips, and Sam answered, "Coffee and a burger. Want anything?"

Joe smiled. "Gonna lose that girlish figure if you're not careful. No, I'm good. Just make sure you get some rest, okay?"

"Will do. See you in a while." He skipped the bank of pay phones outside this time and went into the diner. He'd spotted a phone there the night before, and this time he preferred not having anyone from inside the hotel looking at him while he made his call.

Evelyn Hope answered on the third ring.

"A couple of teenage girls will come by tomorrow. Not long after they check everything out, the whole group is supposed to show."

"How many of you are there?"

For a second he thought about lying and then decided against it. Her people had already met them once. "Five.

Three boys, two girls."

"Anything else?"

"Yes. We'll be armed." He almost said Joe's name and decided against it, though he wasn't really sure why. "Subject Seven wants to meet you. If he can't, he'll take your people hostage and torture them for the information."

"Thank you, Sam. See you tomorrow." She killed the connection after that without giving him a chance to respond.

And just like that it was done. Gene was Jewish and had never read the Bible. Sam didn't care either way, but he'd heard a name before that rang in his mind as if it were being whispered in his ear.

"Judas."

He did his best to ignore that voice as he sat at the table and waited for his meal. He wasn't very hungry, but Joe might still be watching. Best to make it look good.

When the food came, his stomach grumbled and Sam ate the food with the appetite he thought was missing. Apparently treachery was hungry work.

Chapter Twenty-Two

Cody Laurel

WITH THE MORNING CAME a very large breakfast, courtesy of Joe Bronx. It seemed that in his travels, he had found almost every place on the planet that had good food, and the Chicago area was no exception.

Cody was feeling better, enough so that he ate and ate well. When they were done consuming enough food for a football team, Joe laid out the situation for everyone.

"What I need from you ladies is simple. Just go down the street and look at the houses. See if anyone's home. They shouldn't be. If the coast is clear, we hit the house and wait for them."

Cody frowned. He couldn't say with any sincerity that he thought of himself as a human lie detector, but he wasn't so sure about Joe's words here. They smacked of half-truths. Still, the large, hairy man who killed bears with his empty hands wasn't going to get called on it. Not by him at least. He was feeling better, but not cocky enough to commit suicide.

"And if anyone's there?" Tina looked at her empty plate with regret.

"Then all the better. That means we'll have less time to wait around for them to get to us."

"How do you plan on winning this?" Cody looked at Joe and then quickly looked away. Though he'd been doing well while they were eating, now he was feeling a little green.

"Simple. They're going to be looking for me and the rest of the soldiers. That's what we're going to give them. Only this time, we'll have weapons."

Cody looked back toward him. "You think that'll make a difference?"

"Absolutely." Joe smiled. "Last time they wanted to take us alive. If they hadn't, I think they'd have been using all that artillery they had with them. I bet the same is true this time. So we go in hard and fast. I want them alive too, but I'm okay with them being dead." He looked from one person to the next, not letting his eyes linger too long on Kyrie. "I'd like to ask one of them some questions, but I can survive without the extra information."

Tina shook her head. "No disrespect and all of that, but this is just stupid. Why not just go in with our hands over our heads and surrender if all you want is to meet Evelyn Hope?"

Before Joe even answered, Tina'd gone back to looking at her hands. She had chops. Cody would have wet himself even asking that question, though it had been in the back of his mind.

Joe stared at the top of Tina's head like he was willing her to look at him, but she didn't bother and eventually he was forced to answer or look like an ass in front of everyone.

"We need to see Evelyn Hope. If this is her house, and it might be, then awesome and we'll wait. If it's a trap, and it probably is, then we get a few of them and we get the information we need from them about where she is and how we can find her."

"How long you been on your own, Tarzan?"

"Excuse me?" Joe seemed almost to swell with anger.

Tina looked up from her hand—which seemed to have become an object of endless fascination for her—and stared hard at Joe. "If all you want is Evelyn Hope and we run into those guys, and if those guys are the ones who can lead us to Evelyn Hope, why not surrender and avoid the possible bloodshed?" Tina's eyes trailed up and down him with cold contempt, her expression saying very clearly that she thought he was being stupid. "Let me put it another way: what if they feel the same way about us?"

"That we're expendable?"

"Yeah."

"Then I guess we just better be meaner than they are." He smiled at her and stared until she looked away, her face just starting to blush.

Cody watched her become unsettled by the way Joe looked. To hide how much the scrutiny flustered her, Tina stood up and dusted her jeans with her hands in case anything was sticking to the denim. "Fine. We'll play it your way. This time. So come on, Kyrie. Let's get this done."

Kyrie nodded. "But I've got an idea."

Tina didn't even look at her. "Tell me on the way."

They left the room and Kyrie did her best to keep up with Tina's pace.

Chapter Twenty-Three

Kyrie Merriwether/Not-Kyrie

KYRIE FELT THE WIND blowing across her face and savored the sensation for a moment. The pavement was smooth under the wheels of the freshly stolen—by Tina, who had no problem with theft, not by Kyrie, who was terrified of getting caught—bicycle, and she coasted smoothly down the slight hill leading to the edge of Sullivan Street.

Her clothes were slightly baggy and smelled of stale cigarettes and staler perfume. Somewhere along the way, around the same time their Others had stolen the motorcycles, they'd stolen some clothes too. Leather and denim. How ludicrous they must have looked, two little girls wearing the regalia of a motorcycle club while pedaling away on their Schwinns.

The houses were all nice enough, but the area felt wrong. Maybe that was because she knew it was supposed to be a trap for her Other and the rest of the monsters. No one knew who she was, so she was supposedly safe doing this.

There were people around. That was one thing. Not just grown-ups, but kids and teenagers around her age. There were a lot of people. She shook her head. It was almost like a block party, there were so many people.

And that was the thing that bothered her. There were too many people, even for a weekend day. She'd never been anywhere in her life with so many people lounging around outside the houses rather than inside their homes. People had chores or homework or jobs, and that meant you didn't see them just hanging around. But here, on Sullivan Street, there were teens sitting at the porch of the place two houses down from the address she and Tina were supposed to look at. And across the street were three men working on trimming bushes and mowing the lawn. There wasn't enough of a lawn for one man, let alone three.

It looked casual, but in a forced way. Like it was supposed to look as much like a normal neighborhood as it could, but the extras they'd hired for the shot were all trying too hard.

She slid her eyes over to Tina and saw the other girl looking back at her. She had the same feeling; Kyrie could see it in her expression. Tina stood up from the seat of her bike and pedaled faster. Sooner or later the bikes were going to be missed, and Kyrie wanted to return them before that happened.

She pedaled harder as well. They'd seen enough.

A mile later, they dropped the bikes on the lawn of a house that was close to the one where they'd snagged them. Some fingers would maybe be pointed at neighbors who were innocent, but if the owners of the bikes were awake and had noticed them missing, they couldn't bring them back to the right spot without a confrontation. No way she wanted that. She couldn't trust that her Other would behave if she was confronted.

Tina pulled another disposable cell phone from her pocket and dialed quickly. Kyrie watched and felt a little amusement. The girl had purchased half a dozen phones before they ever met, and every time she made phone calls, she got rid of the last phone and activated a new one. She was down to two phones left. She'd have to buy more soon or learn to get over her paranoia. Tina tilted her head a bit and looked down the street with an impatient expression until the call was answered. "Yeah. There's people all over the place. It's a setup." She nodded. "We're waiting on you. We got our motorcycles and we'll get 'em started."

Kyrie frowned. They had been okay on the bicycles, but driving the motorcycles over had been a bit challenging. The things weighed more than she'd ever expected and they were designed for big biker types, not teenage girls. After the group realized who the motorcycles belonged to, they'd talked about getting rid of them. But in the end Gene suggested saving them and hiding them in a copse of woods not far from the hotel. They might need transportation in a hurry. Turned out he was right.

Tina'd just cut off the phone when the mental call came. *Wake up!*

And as soon as they heard it, their bodies responded. Kyrie felt the Other waking, moving inside her mind, swimming up from whatever depths she hid in, and felt her lips peel back in a smile of anticipation. Her body, but not hers. Her mind, but not hers anymore. The Other was coming fast and furious, and the pain of her muscles twisting and changing hit her as the darkness came to sweep her away.

Three feet away, Tina hissed in frustration and then laughed as her voice changed.

And then they were gone, replaced by two different girls, who moved away from the discarded bikes and headed for the motorcycles that they'd stowed when they arrived. Joe Bronx spoke in their heads, telling them where the bikes were. Even as he led them to their rides, they could hear the other motorcycles coming, heading in their direction.

They came around the corner hard and fast, three heavily muscled animals in leather. Though they were all young, they looked as vicious as the people they'd stolen the bikes from in the first place. They wore helmets to hide their features, and so the girls put on their helmets as well. This was as close as they were getting to being disguised.

Confusion was an enemy when they first woke up, but Joe was there to make it better. He was strong and smart, and they couldn't help but admire him. He'd saved them from eternal slumber, and that alone would have earned their loyalty, but even now he kept them aware of everything that was happening.

It was only a matter of moments before they were riding together, heading for Sullivan Street and ready to finish the madness, ready to be freed from the prisons that their counterparts made of their lives.

How much better everything would have been for all involved if they hadn't already been betrayed.

Chapter Twenty-Four

Evelyn Hope

"THEY'RE COMING." EVELYN HEARD the Rafael's voice softly through her headset. She watched the monitors and felt herself tense. There was a preposterous number of cameras set in the area, because there had to be. The entire neighborhood was a setup, a dummy placed for the purpose of seeing how well the Doppelgangers adjusted to life in a suburban environment. If she'd learned anything from the past, it was that privacy could not be allowed. Subject Seven had taught them that lesson, and it had been costly. Now she was grateful for the extra security and the technology that allowed them to have so many cameras and microphones hidden in plain sight.

All of the people who'd been on the street, waiting, looking around and acting as normal as possible, immediately moved for cover. They were trained—and well trained at that—but they were not here to fight. They were here to observe and to offer backup only if absolutely necessary. This was a test. Who was better at being a Doppelganger? Seven or the Strike Team? Evelyn had to know. She had to see for herself if everything they'd been working for was a successful endeavor when compared to the monster that had come before the Strike Teams.

She watched the Strikers ready themselves. The last time they'd been taken off guard. No one to blame but themselves, and they understood that. They had been told that their enemies were faster than humans, that they were actually on par with the Strikers, but it hadn't registered. Hearing it hadn't meant believing it. Now they had seen and felt it for themselves.

Rafael let them know it was time—reminded them that this time, failure would mean dire consequences. Perhaps a few of them might have wanted to argue, but they'd been better trained than that. It had to be done. They had to win this. There could be no excuses.

"Mary, Declan, Tori . . . Hit them from the left. Sean and Heather, wait for my mark." He was talking into the radio headsets instead of using his mental commands for two reasons. First, because that way Evelyn could hear everything going on, and second, because they weren't one hundred percent sure that Seven couldn't eavesdrop on whatever mental commands he issued. There were still too many things they didn't know about Seven and how he'd evolved over the last five years. Most Alphas couldn't read the thoughts of anyone who wasn't a part of their birth clutch, but that was because they'd been designed that way. Subject Seven and his friends were prototypes: they were unpredictable.

Evelyn watched them coming, heard the Strikers murmur their assent and waited. And they came, five forms moving at high speed, riding motorcycles that had been built with speed in mind.

The street was empty, of course, which was why they'd chosen this location.

She'd have killed to see their faces, but the five wore helmets with visors. They didn't so much stop and park as they climbed from bikes that were still rolling. The vehicles staggered and crashed to the ground, and as they did, the five figures who'd been riding them moved toward the address they'd been given.

"Now. Take them now." Rafael's voice was calm, in control.

Mary fired from the left, the long cables from her Taser spinning madly as darts shot straight at the one who'd shot her before. He moved quickly, but not quite as fast as he might have wished. One of the barbs bounced off his jacket, but the other sank deep enough to catch his attention and merit a yelp of pain. He didn't even bother turning his head. Instead his hand wrapped around the wire feed and he yanked hard. Mary had two choices: she could let go of the Taser or she could get hauled from her hiding spot. She took option number three and ran at him, screaming like a demon the entire way.

Disorientation was a tactic they used regularly. Every last one of the strangers turned to look at Mary as she came toward them at high speed, shrieking as she moved.

And while they were looking, Declan nailed the biggest one of them with a riot stick across the back of his head. The hard wood broke on impact and the helmet cracked, but the blow was solid and the giant fell forward and landed on his face. He might have been thinking about getting up, but if so, his body wasn't listening. The big boy stayed down.

They had two females with them, and both of them moved at the same time, one sliding into a defensive stance, the other charging at Declan like she had a chance in hell of taking him down. Tori fired her Taser at the one moving for Declan, but the girl was fast enough to lower her head, and both of the darts skimmed across the top of her helmet as she changed her trajectory and headed for Tori.

"Tori! Look out!" Rafael called his warning and Tori's head shook with irritation. Evelyn knew right then, of course. Tori and Rafael had been fooling around, just as she'd suspected. Rafael was in the wrong, too. Just because they'd made out a few times didn't suddenly mean he had to protect her. Tori was ridiculously skilled at hand-to-hand combat.

"I've got this!" Tori's voice lashed out even as she dropped and drove her foot into the other girl's face. The helmet on her target's head shattered on impact and sent the girl staggering back into the bushes.

Evelyn felt a swell of pride. Damn right, she had it.

Mary let out a scream, and Evelyn switched to a different screen, catching the action as best she could. So much was happening at once! The one Mary had attacked was fighting back and he was very, very angry. Evelyn could see the red marks where Mary had hit him, but he wasn't going down. It had to be unsettling for the Strike Team, running across enemies who were so damned tough.

Declan hurdled the body of the one he'd taken down and prepared to attack the last of the males, the one who was looking at him with a small, playful smile. He shouldn't have been smiling. Declan was a wrecking machine.

The girl next to him interceded, dropping close to the ground and sweeping her leg out to knock his feet out from under him. Declan hopped, easily moving out of the way of her leg.

Then the big bruiser he'd knocked flat came off the ground like a freshly launched rocket and slammed Declan into the side of the house they'd been approaching.

"Shit!" Evelyn shook her head. Cocky. Declan was getting too cocky again. He had to watch that.

"Let's move. They need us." Rafael spoke softly. Evelyn resisted the urge to make comments of her own; this was an observational situation and she needed to know what the Strike Team could do without help.

They came from behind the house and charged at the backs of the remaining targets. Sean didn't hesitate. The behemoth who'd half broken him against the van was standing up and reaching for Tori, but Sean got there first, using two of the riot sticks to defend himself and attack at the same time.

The big boy never had a chance. Declan had already hurt him, and that was enough to give Sean the edge. He slapped one of the sticks against the ape's left knee—the one holding all of his weight at that instant—and as he fell forward, Sean used the other wooden club to strike him in his throat. The bruiser fell down, gasping, unable to catch his breath.

At the same time, Tori attacked the girl who'd been defending their leader.

Evelyn felt her pulse increase. Their leader. Subject Seven. The monster himself. They hesitated. Her Strikers slowed for just a moment. They weren't supposed to be impressed by him, but maybe they couldn't help being in awe of the one that got away. Subject Seven was the one the rest of them were patterned after. He'd been tested and studied until they knew his weaknesses and strengths, until they could determine that he was the best of the previous generation of Doppelgangers. Strong, fast, intelligent.

And then he'd disappeared. Either taken by force or escaping on his own, he'd disappeared. Evelyn knew what happened, of course, but the Strike Teams were not told that he'd forced his way from the compound. Best not to give them any ideas. And now they could get him back for her. They could see exactly how he had changed, what had happened to the best of the previous model.

Rafael moved carefully, observing his enemy. Subject Seven looked back at him, that same half smile playing around his mouth. He was hard. He carried himself with unsettling confidence and looked at Rafael the same way a parent looks at a toddler, like he wasn't even close to being a threat.

"I remember you." Subject Seven ignored all of the fighters around them and focused on Rafael. He returned the favor. His people would win. He knew that.

Evelyn watched her Strike Team moving, fighting, winning. Even Declan was getting back up, too tough to be easily knocked out.

Rafael's voice came over the radio. "I'm gonna kick your ass."

Subject Seven bared his teeth in a smile and gestured for him to come forward. "Bring it."

There was a gun in the belt of Rafael's target. Subject Seven didn't reach for it. Instead he waited for Rafael to come to him.

Rafael did not disappoint. He charged, already assessing exactly where and how he would hit his enemy. Subject Seven had left an opening. His left side was begging to get hit, and so Rafael swung a hard jab toward his ribs and then staggered back as Seven's fist smashed into his face like a sledgehammer.

Evelyn flinched as surely as if she'd felt the blow herself. Her son was being stupid and cocky, and before he could recover from the first punch, Seven hit him again, driving him back toward the street. He stumbled as he backed up and almost lost his balance. And as he compensated, Subject Seven brought his foot up and kicked him square in the family jewels.

Rafael went down. He groaned and caught himself on his hands before his face crashed into the lawn, his eyes looking around hastily, taking in the situation. The numbers were in their favor and the Strike Team had taken down their enemies. He could see the biggest of the lot still trying to breathe, the other male on the ground unconscious and one of the girls flattened as well.

And then Subject Seven kicked him in the head and he fell backward, overcome by excruciating pain.

Subject Seven looked down at him; that half smile had returned.

Rafael smiled back. He still had the upper hand. Subject Seven was cocky too.

"The king is in his court; the gates are closed and winter comes too soon to us." Rafael said the words exactly as he'd been taught them and Subject Seven stared at him with wide, wild eyes.

"What did you—?" Then Seven fell backward, his hands moving to clutch at the sides of his head.

The brute, the violent monster who had once upon a time gone on a killing spree as he freed himself from a hidden compound—the stuff of nightmares—went down then, unable to scream as his body convulsed.

By the time Rafael climbed to his feet, Subject Seven was gone, replaced by a thinner boy—still muscular, still athletic, but so much smaller than Seven—who looked at him with confusion.

Before the boy could so much as ask a question, Rafael's Taser darts punched into his stomach. He screamed when Rafael triggered the charge.

Evelyn closed her eyes against the sound of Bobby's pain.

Her team bagged their enemies with ease, tying their wrists with heavy nylon zip ties and binding their ankles as well. And as they finished, Rafael spoke through their radio connection, smiling as he told her that their quarry had been captured and would soon be brought in.

Then Mary told him that one of the girls was missing and

Evelyn felt her blood pressure rise slightly.

One of them had gotten away.

They fanned out quickly, looking for the one who'd fled the fight, but had no success.

One of the five they'd been sent to retrieve was missing.

The good news was that Subject Seven was secured. In the long run, that was the part that mattered the most to Evelyn Hope. And what she wanted, she got.

Chapter Twenty-Five

Not-Tina

WHAT A DIFFERENCE A day makes.

The Failures were captured, it was true, with only one exception. That single individual made her way back to the hotel as soon as she'd lost the helmet and the jacket. Without them, she was just a girl in the eyes of most people. Her jeans, shoes, and baby doll tee were nondescript enough to let her make it to safety without any of the Strikers recognizing her. That was good, because she thought she saw one of the males giving her the eye at one point, though he was too far away to be certain. Despite the temptation to confront him, she kept her cool and kept going.

That's the spirit. It's up to you now. You have to get us free. The voice in her head was still there, and she took an odd comfort from that fact. She hated running, would have preferred to stay and break a few heads, but the voice told her it was best to have someone in backup and that she was the best choice. She was the most likely to get away and then come back to fix everything.

She dug into the pocket of her jeans and found her hotel room key. A moment later she was inside the room and could relax. She looked at the snake tattoo on her arm. In hindsight it might have been a mistake. It was a damned large identifying mark and at least one of the enemies had seen her, had taken in the colorful markings.

Not-Tina looked at herself in the mirror as she flopped on the bed. "Guess I'll just have to kill him the next time I see him."

They'd hit her hard and fast and she'd landed in the shrubs as the combat started in earnest. Not-Tina was just starting to get back up when Joe's voice suggested that she hide away and see what happened. She'd listened, because so far Joe had never let her down.

It'd been easy to get away. Her Other was skilled at moving quietly, at not being seen when she wanted to hide, a necessary talent when your dear mother liked to hit.

Despite everything, she smiled at the thought of Tina's mom being pulled out of the water, dead and bloated. Tina had loved the woman. Not-Tina was not as forgiving of anyone that struck at her or at her Other.

She turned on the TV to have some background noise while she thought about what to do next. She was waiting for Joe, really, because she had no idea where the others were, where they had been taken, and she needed to know that before she could help them. And she would help them, of course, because she needed them. She wanted to have them around. Tina might think she could get through the world without anyone else, but Not-Tina wanted someone to watch her back. She'd made enemies and she'd need a little help to finish what she had started.

The news was on. Good old Hunter liked to keep up on the current events. She was just toying with the idea of changing channels when Gene's face showed up on the screen. In the picture he was smiling, which was a pretty alien expression on his face from what little she'd seen of him.

She turned up the volume and listened. The story was just starting.

The woman on the TV was prattling on about state-of-the-art technologies, and as she spoke, the image changed to a still shot of Gene wearing the clothes he'd had on yesterday—Not-Tina paused for a second, wondering how the woman could know that, and then pushed the thought away. It wasn't important, not really. Next to him was Kyrie, and the two of them were carrying bags of food.

"Little late on that. Not gonna find them with that picture."

Restless. She couldn't sit still. It didn't matter that she was tired or hungry—she was always hungry—she was feeling confined in the room.

Of course if she left the room, she would have to take money and a few weapons. Also, she'd need a place to go.

The announcer was talking about the video confirmation again, stating that as of yesterday Eugene Rothstein was definitely in Chicago and reminding the viewers that the Rothstein family had offered a huge reward for his safe return.

Under different circumstances she might have been tempted to get the reward—she had a lot of money, yes, but most of it was still stashed wherever Joe had hidden it in Boston—but currently Gene was unavailable for delivery.

"Oh well. Guess I'll just have to earn it the old-fashioned way if I need more." She was thinking of Paulo Scarabelli when she said it, remembering that she'd already taken a fortune from him and that she had every intention of ruining him. Remembering his anger made her feel better. But it was remembering Tony Parmiatti that made her smile and kill the TV. Tony hurt her Other in ways no one else ever had. Making him suffer was her pleasure.

It took a minute, because it always took her a little time to access Tina's memories. She sorted through a lifetime of nonsense that meant nothing to her, the people and memories that made up Tina's sum. It was like speed reading an entire encyclopedia for the right vague clues to get what she wanted, but she finally managed to recall the times cute little Tony bragged about his business trips and his contacts all around the country.

It was amazing that he even had a job. He'd talked enough in front of a little fifteen-year-old kid to get him and half the mob convicted if Tina had ever offered information to the Feds. Guys would do anything if they thought they were going to get lucky.

Tina, she never understood that. Not-Tina was a different story. She knew about power. She respected the process.

A slow, sadistic smile spread across her face and she quickly changed her clothes as she started planning. Long sleeves this time, because that ink needed to not be seen.

Tony talked a lot. Way more than he should have.

She didn't have all the details, but with just a little work she was sure she could get what she needed from the local mobsters—there were always people who had information—and, more importantly, people who could get her weapons. Even if she had to break a few heads to get it.

And then there was that guy who'd sent the letter to Evelyn Hope. The others had talked about him, how maybe he was a link. What was the name? Ah, Joshua Warburton. That was it.

"Hey, Josh. Wanna show me where your friends like to hide?" She didn't expect him to answer, as she was talking only to hear herself speak and they hadn't met yet. But they would, just as soon as she had what she needed.

Chapter Twenty-Six

Evelyn Hope

"SO TELL ME WHAT you have so far, gentlemen." Evelyn stared at the wall without seeing any of the diplomas or certificates that adorned it. She didn't need to study any of that nonsense. She already knew that Josh was a super-genius. He was almost her equal, which said a lot, really.

George opened his mouth and then closed it. Josh was in charge here, and George would let him speak.

Josh took his meerschaum pipe from his mouth and set it on the desk. He'd quit smoking years earlier, but now and then he still gnawed on the thing when he had a strong desire for a smoke or when he was wound up. He was currently wound as tightly as a precision watch spring.

"Where to start." Josh looked at the notepad in his left hand and nodded. "First, we have four of them. That means it's possible one of them got away. Not sure about that, but by your earlier reports there were possibly as many as five, and there were certainly five bikes on the scene of their capture."

Evelyn held up a hand. "My insider told me there were five. We'll work under the assumption that we might have one still out there and keep our ears to the ground. What else is going on?"

Josh moved on. "First, one of them is likely going to die within the next week. I've never seen this, but you have. Remember when we first started having successes, there were a few of the subjects that had such gross differences in size that the changes caused them permanent damage?"

Evelyn nodded.

"Well, one of them is showing all the same symptoms. High fever, delirium, no sign of actual infection but a lot of the side effects that would indicate a severe case of influenza or pneumonia."

Evelyn nodded again, interested now. She'd never seen the changes in any Doppelganger beyond the age of two. "Film it. I want to see every stage of this, please. I want to know what to expect if it should happen to one of ours."

Josh made a note. George stared at her with an unreadable expression for a moment and then made himself look away as she returned the gaze. He tended to forget that she was a scientist first. Was it cruel to watch a teenager die and suffer? Yes, but she needed to know if there was any way to stop the destructive changes that occurred in some of the early Doppelgangers. There was only one way to find out, and the first stage of that learning was observation.

Because the look he'd cast her way made her feel just a bit defensive—a sensation she hated—Evelyn turned to George and explained. "Back in the very early stages of the Doppelganger program there were at least a dozen of the first successes that simply rejected the changes. Near as we have been able to figure it out, it's like a body rejecting an organ transplant, but on a whole-body scale. The changes are simply too significant, and the shifting genetic codes that allow two bodies to exist in one place go sour. We still haven't figured out exactly why it happens or how to stop it, but by observing this case, we might finally get a few breaks to avoid the problem in the future." George gave her a tentative smile.

She went back to ignoring him.

"What about the rest of them?" She directed the question to Josh.

"We already did the surgeries. Everything went well and there probably won't even be any noticeable scars for them to run across. Subject Seven has been isolated. We've given him a very heavy dose of the blanket drugs. They seem to be working, but we won't know for certain until he changes back into Subject Seven. Just to be safe, we'll dose him again before he wakes completely."

"Which form is he currently in?" She thought she understood, but wanted to make sure. She didn't want to get stressed more than she had to.

Josh didn't look at her. "Bobby."

Evelyn kept her face neutral. Bobby. Her son. She didn't dare get her hopes up.

"Evelyn . . ."

"Tell me."

"We don't know all of the details, but there was an accident at some time in the past. A bad one. There was serious head trauma."

"What?" Her ears were ringing. There had been a time when she could count on Bobby's phone calls. When he stopped, she'd assumed the worse, but maybe the head trauma would explain a few things.

"Evelyn, there's a very real chance that Bobby doesn't even exist anymore. We just don't know for certain."

She directed her gaze back toward the wall.

Josh put a hand on her shoulder. "That doesn't mean anything, not yet. You have to meet him and see."

Chapter Twenty-Seven

Hunter Harrison

HUNTER'S HEAD FELT two sizes too big, and if he had to guess, it weighed just a little less than an aircraft carrier. His mouth was too dry and his eyes were stinging like he'd been in a dust storm. He moved to wipe at his eyes and was stopped by the handcuffs locking him into a metal hospital bed.

That woke him right up. He opened his eyes and looked around. He was in a white room with white furniture and fluorescent lights that were bright enough to make his eyes water. At least that helped with the dusty feeling.

To his left and above his head he could hear the steady sounds of a heart monitor letting him know that he was still alive. Despite the belief that he had never been near a heart monitor, he had a strong sense of déjà vu. *Must be Joe's memories,* he mused. *Joe's the one they used to check on all the time, isn't he?*

It didn't take a genius to figure out that things had gone down the wrong way. He slowly turned his head and looked at the room in greater detail. One door, metal with a heavy lock. One mirrored window. He could look at it and tell it was a two-way mirror. It was built into the wall instead of just hanging, and the tint was wrong. It didn't give back a light enough reflection. Once again, he had to guess it was Joe's memories helping him understand. That thought bothered the hell out of him.

What bothered him even more was that he could feel Joe Bronx in his head, like a pressure that was slowly building. He closed his eyes for a moment and pushed back: he was the strong one. He had to be if there was any chance that he could have a life. A moment later the pressure faded down again.

The door opened and a young teenager came into the room, moving with military precision. The kid's back was ramrod straight and his shoulders were squared, his hair cut military short. There was something familiar about him, though, something that sent gooseflesh across Hunter's skin and made his eyes water a second time. He heard his heartbeat increase.

The word snuck out of his mouth as he saw the other boy's lower lip tremble and his eyes water. "G-Gabby?" The name felt right. "Gabe, is that you?"

"Bobby? You remember me?" His voice shook.

Bobby? Who the hell was Bobby? Was that his real name? He'd never been sure about Hunter.

"I sort of do . . ." His voice trailed off. Small flashes of the boy in front of him, but he was too old, had grown so much. "I can't remember everything."

Before the boy could answer, the door opened a second time and the woman came into the room. He recognized her instantly, of course. One look at her face and the memories hit him like a tidal wave, slamming into him and washing over him. Her touch, her smile, her fingers moving through his hair. The press of her lips against his forehead as she tucked him into bed at night, a hundred different bedtime stories, the hot cocoa she would make when it was cold outside and he was coming home from school. There were memories, oh yes, so many more than he had ever expected. Seeing her broke down the doors that had hidden them away. Not all of the doors, but enough to leave him speechless for almost a minute as he looked at her and tried to reconcile the hard lines on her face with the woman he had last seen five years earlier. Her hair was too short, her stance too stiff. She wasn't smiling, and her eyes seemed so worried as they looked him over.

"Mom?" How could one word hold so much weight?

"Bobby. It's good to see you." Her voice was tight in her throat, barely released. She moved toward him and he shivered as with a fever. This was too much. This was his world, or at least the parts that mattered. The rest of it wasn't important. But this? This was . . . well, this was everything.

Except.

"Where's Dad? Is he here too?" He could feel his father's strong arms scooping him up when he was younger, swinging him in a half circle before he set him down. Such a big man, like a giant in his memories.

He tried to sit up and finally managed, despite the thick cuffs on his wrists. The cuffs the cops had used were substantially thinner.

His mom looked at him looking at his wrists. "We had to, Bobby." Her voice broke a bit, apologetic, sad, but still with a stern edge that he remembered, oh, how well he remembered it and all out of nowhere.

"I know." He looked away. "He's still inside me." His stomach clenched at that thought. He didn't know much about Joe Bronx, but he knew that his Other hated him. If he ever got a chance to get his hands on Gabby or his mom . . . "Can you get rid of him? Can you make me just me, Mom?"

Even as he spoke, he felt Joe inside him, stirring, trying to wake up like a bear coming out of a deep, hibernating slumber.

"I don't know." She looked at him for a long moment and then she looked away. "But I'm going to try."

Hunter—Bobby still felt wrong—clenched his teeth and

fought back the wall of gray that was trying to overwhelm him. He was tired, and it was hard to fight against Joe when he was tired.

Her words struggled past the strain of fighting Joe off, but he succeeded for the moment. Joe faded away like a bad memory.

Hunter thought about his mother's words and felt a coldness in the pit of his stomach. He wanted to believe her. He did. But her words felt like a lie.

Chapter Twenty-Eight

Kyrie Merriwether

KYRIE WOKE UP IN restraints, strapped to a metal table, with thickly padded handcuffs on her wrists and similar cuffs around her ankles. One look told her Gene and Cody were in the same boat on either side of her.

Kyrie looked to her left and saw Gene looking at her. His face was almost expressionless, but his eyes were deeply troubled.

To her right, Cody lay on his examination table and shivered, his teeth chattering even though he was asleep or at least unconscious. His skin was pale and sweaty and his hair was soaked through to the point that he could have just climbed out of a swimming pool.

"So. I could be wrong, but I think we screwed up." Gene's voice made her look back toward him. Unlike Cody, he seemed uninjured.

Kyrie shifted her arms and legs, unconsciously testing the amount of give in the restraints. She had about six inches of play on each limb. Not much, but better than nothing.

The room was large enough to accommodate all three tables and little else. There were heart monitors and several other sensors attached to each of them. She was wearing a jumpsuit that was loose but comfortable, same as the others. They all came in the same nondescript shade of gray. Her personal clothes and her shoes were gone. She had no idea where.

While she contemplated the mystery of her new fashions, the door to the room opened and in came five people that made her feel a bit uneasy. She didn't remember meeting them, but that didn't mean she hadn't. She was only around part of the time.

The five seemed around the same age as her, but it was hard to say for certain. The way they walked, the way they looked—she had to guess that they were Others. Their grace was disturbing, not quite human.

One of them, a male, moved closer to her and looked her up and down without saying a word. His gaze made her uncomfortable.

"What the hell are you staring at?" She had just been seriously thinking about asking that very question, but it was Cody that voiced the concern. She looked his way. He was awake, sort of. His lips were almost blue, and if she hadn't known better, she'd have thought for certain that he'd almost drowned.

The one who'd been eyeing her looked toward Cody and sneered. "Not much, loser. Just a bunch of wannabes."

One of the girls looked toward each of them with wide eyes. "You shouldn't even exist. I mean, seriously, you aren't even possible."

Gene answered. "We must be possible. We're right here. Way I heard it, someone was supposed to dispose of us and sent us out for adoption instead."

The girl moved closer to him, staring with the sort of scrutiny that made Gene uncomfortable. He looked away from her eyes, blushing. "But how did you change?" she asked. "There are command words."

"What are those?" Kyrie frowned at the other girl.

"Command words, phrases . . ." The girl looked shocked that she wouldn't know. "The words that can make you change."

"We don't have those." Kyrie spoke softly and frowned a bit. There was a distant memory, like something she was trying to remember from a dream, of Joe falling down after the one who wasn't with this group said something to him. Was that what they meant by command words? She didn't know. She couldn't know. She hadn't been there. That had been Not-Kyrie. Just thinking about it made her head hurt.

Cody let out a deep moan and looked away from them.

His voice was deeper when he spoke. "I remember you butt faces. Get out of here. I don't want to see you."

"Watch your mouth, loser." The first one that had spoken to them took a step closer. "I still owe you. Don't give me a reason."

The girl put her hand on his shoulder. "Don't. We aren't even supposed to be here."

Kyrie understood. They were curious. They wanted to see the freaks. "Get a good look and get out." She looked away from them too, oddly humiliated. She never thought of herself as a freak, and certainly not a freak among a small army of other genetic anomalies.

"And if we don't? What will you do about it if we stay right here?" That was the boy again. He liked to lead with his chin when he was trying to be tough.

"Tell the people who come in next that you were here." Gene's voice was calm and logical as he spoke. "I bet they don't like it when you disobey. I bet they punish you. Want that? Want to get punished?"

Half of them looked shocked, like the idea never really crossed their minds. The mouthy one looked like he was ready to say something again, but the girl stopped him. Finally he sneered and nodded. "We won. That's all that matters."

The voice that came from Cody sounded more like his Other than him. "Keep telling yourself that, loser.

I remember knocking you halfway through a van."

The girl held her friend back when he started to lunge at Cody. Only he wasn't Cody anymore, not really. He was changing, his body growing, swelling with muscle and larger bones. The transformation wasn't complete and it looked uncomfortable.

A moment later they all left the room and Kyrie stared at the mirrored wall, wondering if they were still out there, still watching from a safe distance. She looked toward Cody and saw his body was still changing, and he was grunting in discomfort. It had to hurt, didn't it? The way his bones were growing and shrinking, pulling and twisting the muscles with them.

"Cody?" He didn't answer. "Hank? What's happening to you?"

"I think I'm dying. I can't control it anymore." He mumbled the words, and in the reflection she saw that his eyes were closed again. He settled back on the examination table, and it groaned in protest at his changing weight.

After that he was silent, and neither she nor Gene had any words of comfort to offer.

Chapter Twenty-Nine

Evelyn Hope

EVELYN SENT GABRIEL AWAY before the change took place. She had to send him away, because she didn't want him to see her cry.

She could sense it. Subject Seven was waking up, whether she wanted him to or not.

George and Josh were the ones that spoke to her in the observation room, explained in soft, caring voices that the MRI and ultrasounds had revealed substantial trauma to Bobby's skull. The damage was old, and the scans showed significant areas of scar tissue. That would explain his amnesia. But the pictures also revealed the impossible: regrowth. His brain was healing itself. It was a slow process, but it was happening.

The only problem? Gray matter wasn't supposed to come back from trauma. Once brain cells were dead, they didn't recover. Not in humans, anyway.

They'd set out to design better soldiers, better spies, dual forms in one body. They'd succeeded and that made her happy. But looking at the severe damage and the new growth made her wonder if they hadn't gone too far. What was that old adage from all the black-and-white science-fiction movies? Oh yes, they warned against playing God.

What did I create? The thought crept through her and her skin crawled. She loved Bobby and was grateful that he was recovering, but what did that say about Subject Seven, who was always the physically stronger of the two?

So yes, Gabriel left. Evelyn made sure he was far away from his brother before Subject Seven came back into existence. And because she was a cautious sort, she studied him from behind the two-way mirror for a while before she considered entering the room.

George and Josh stood next to her, both of them looking at her as much as they looked at her pet monster. And there was no mistaking it: he was a monster.

As Seven woke up, he looked around the small room and then to the glass barrier that separated them. Two-way mirrors are simple enough. On one side is a mirror. On the other side the glass is transparent so that an observer can watch the reactions of whoever is looking into the mirror without being seen.

Subject Seven must have understood the concept, because

he looked at the glass that showed him nothing but his own reflection and he grinned.

"I can smell you over there, 'Mother.' " He tried his restraints, tested them, but casually. He didn't thrash around as she'd half expected him to. She wasn't worried. The bonds had been designed with him in mind. They'd been tested many times before. "Did you have a chance to see your precious Bobby? Did you have a nice little reunion?"

She didn't answer. Instead she kept looking at him as the emotions tried to break through. There was pride in her heart when she saw him: because he was hers, he was the key that allowed them to proceed with the amazing things they had accomplished even after he escaped. But far greater than that pride, there was anger and hurt. The thing in front of her took her Bobby and had killed her husband, Tom. They'd meant so much to her—Bobby for being the sweet and wonderful boy he was, and Tom because no matter what happened in her life, he had been there to comfort her and believe in her. And now they were both gone.

And beyond the anger, the pride, the pain, there was a deep and abiding fear. He was a monster. Subject Seven was savage and smarter than she'd expected. For five years, he'd hidden himself away so well that they couldn't find him, and that was a daunting task: The Janus Corporation had connections all over the world, nearly perfect international radar.

Between the contacts they had in the military and the civilian areas, finding someone was the easiest thing in the world for her. Josh had already located twelve of the families that they were looking for, and that was a very impressive number when you considered that the trail was fifteen years old.

And Seven, oh, so much stronger than anyone had predicted. They'd examined the office building after Rafael's crew had first confronted the orphaned Doppelgangers, and they'd found a stainless steel .38 Special handgun warped into a new shape, crushed by what had seemed to be a bare hand. She didn't know the specifics, but it took a lot more than simple human strength to do that to a handgun—far greater strength than any of the Strike Team Doppelgangers had ever demonstrated. Imagining what that hand could do to soft flesh and human bone was enough to make her skin crawl.

"Oh, come on, Evelyn, I just wanted to talk." And that. He knew she was here. He smelled her. Maybe he even heard how her heartbeat increased when he called her name. His senses were insanely good. She looked toward him, and he was staring in her general direction through the mirror. "I want this over with, Evelyn. I want to have a real life. In exchange for that, I'm willing to make certain allowances."

"Can you believe this kid?" Josh's voice was almost shocking after the silence of their room. "He's strapped to an examination table and getting a feed of drugs that would tranquilize a bear, and he thinks he's in a position to negotiate."

Evelyn watched Seven's reactions on the other side of the glass. She saw him accurately pinpoint exactly where Josh was standing. He stared hard at the spot where Josh's face was, even as the grin spread a little wider on his face.

"You have friends with you, Evelyn. How nice for you. I had friends with me too. Where are they?"

Josh stopped talking. He was getting it. He was understanding at last. Subject Seven wasn't bluffing. He really could smell her.

Seven's eyes stayed on Josh. "Didn't think I was telling the truth, did you? Thought I was lying about smelling Evelyn." He inhaled deeply. "I couldn't forget 'Mother' if I had to. I'm not like Bobby. I have all of my memories intact." The smile he offered was pure poison.

Josh grew paler, his eyes growing wide in his round face. He didn't speak, but he looked to Evelyn and his expression spoke volumes about his fear. The room wasn't airtight, but the idea that one of the things they had created had hearing sensitive enough to detect their whispered discussions put a great deal of their previous communications into a new light. He was thinking exactly what Evelyn herself was thinking: *We can never have another conversation about the Doppelgangers without being in a different building, just in case they might hear us.*

Seven laughed in his cell, and even from a distance she could see his eyes looking from one of them to the next. "Want to come and talk to me now? Want to have a serious discussion about how this is going to play out?"

Evelyn pressed her lips together. Before she could even consider stopping herself, she moved from the observation room and pressed her palm to the ID pad that read her hand and fingerprints and waited while the door slid open.

She stormed into the room with her emotions surging like the tide in a hurricane. Here, this thing, the monster she created, the beast that had killed Tom and taken Bobby away. Here, the demon that had haunted her nightmares ever since he threw her across the room and escaped. Here, in front of her, only now he was bigger than ever, a nightmare given flesh and bone and a sadistic smile. Did he hate her? Did he love her? Fear her? She had no way of knowing anything past the sneering smile he offered as he looked into her eyes, unflinching.

"Here's how this plays out." She hissed the words, her usual calm destroyed by the rage and fear that pushed through her. "You stay here, too drugged to communicate with your new friends. Too weak to escape. While you get to listen in, I'm going to study them. I'm going to see what each of them is capable of. And then when I'm done with them, I'm going to come in here and do the same thing to you." Evelyn was trembling by the time she was done speaking, her muscles tightened to the snapping point, her teeth clenched in hatred. She hadn't let herself think about him, not really, not for a long time. Subject Seven was everything she hated rolled into one bundle and here he was again, his smile unaltered by her rant.

"Well, look at that. A little honesty from you. How refreshing." His voice was low and calm, but she wasn't fooled. Evelyn knew Subject Seven very well indeed. She'd studied him for the first ten years of his life, every day for that time. He was hers, after all—her invention, her creation. If he was the monster, then she was the mad scientist that had to live with creating him. And she knew that Seven was just as angry as she was, but he was better at hiding it than she had ever expected him to be.

"You're never leaving here, Seven. You're here for the rest of your life." She sneered now, and her eyes looked him over, studying the amazing shape of his form, the scars he'd accumulated while living on his own for five years.

"I thought that was a given." He shrugged.

"You haven't figured out the part that matters, boy."

Seven arched an eyebrow and leaned back as best he could on his metal table. "Pray tell."

"I decide how long that life is." Her lips curled slowly into a smile that was as cold as his, and she crossed her arms over her chest. "And I decide how much pain you feel for the entire time I let you live."

The smile on his face crumbled, and for just a moment he let his rage out as well. His teeth actually changed in front of her, growing slightly longer as he roared, "You better be damned sure about that, Evelyn! You better know for certain that I'm never getting away! Because if I do—if I ever manage to break loose again—I'll ruin everything you ever loved!"

"You already did that!" Her voice broke as she screamed and she felt George's hands on her shoulders urging her back, trying to get her out of the room—but she shrugged him off and moved forward, her hand slapping across Seven's mouth, smashing his flesh and drawing blood. "You already took everything away!"

She felt the blood on her fingers along with the spittle that she'd brushed from his mouth with her blow and backed away, realizing exactly how easily he could have taken her fingers had he been fast enough to react. One does not place one's hand in the mouth of a lion.

Instead of roaring anymore, Seven's smile returned, broader than before, though no less sadistic. Pink trails of blood dripped across his teeth as he asked, "How's little Gabby these days?"

George's hands grabbed Evelyn's shoulders again and forcefully pulled her from the room before she could respond. She looked at her second in command with wide eyes and realized she couldn't feel her face. Shock was beginning to set in. Seven did that to her. He got her so rattled she didn't even use the command phrase when she had the chance.

She should have been furious with her personal assistant, but she couldn't be. She was too grateful. For just one moment, she'd been ready to beg for Gabby's life.

Insanity. Gabriel was strong and capable, and his Doppelganger, Rafael, was one of the best soldiers she had ever seen. Surely Subject Seven wouldn't win in a fight between them. Rafael had already bested Seven in combat.

She kept telling herself that as she walked away. Still in the back of her head was that little voice, the one that belonged to the woman who answered to Evvy back when she was far more innocent. That voice kept whispering in her head, asking the question she didn't want to ask: *Who's really the captive here?*

Chapter Thirty

Joe Bronx

JOE CLOSED HIS EYES and listened to the sounds of the people leaving.

He wondered why it was that he hadn't bitten down and taken a few fingers when he had the chance. He should have. Instead of dwelling on it, he ran his tongue across his swollen lips and tasted his own blood. The flesh was already mending, knitting seamlessly back to what it should have been. He'd taken a bullet through his arm a few days ago, and that wound was barely even a memory anymore—just one more scar among many.

He'd riled her. That made him happy in a way that little else did. He was where he wanted to be, but not in the right way. What she'd said was true: he could feel the drugs coursing through his system and try as he might, he couldn't hear the others in his head. Either the drugs were dulling his senses a bit or his new allies were dead. He didn't much like that notion. He should have been able to hear them, to feel them, and there was nothing, and that bothered him more than he wanted to admit, because already he was growing very used to hearing them. They helped keep him calmer.

And they were gone.

And he was alone.

Again.

He shook the thought away. They were expendable. All of them. They were just pawns that he needed to get what he wanted from the world. He didn't dare let them be more than that, because he'd already lost the other Subjects when he was younger, hadn't he? He'd barely survived that. He needed to remember that they were only important as long as he needed them. No feelings, no connections, because those things led to pain that was nearly impossible to get past.

Deep breaths. He made himself stay calm, because losing it wouldn't do him the least bit of good. He'd learned the hard way that he had to have patience to survive in the world. Even when the world was one little room.

This wasn't the way it was supposed to play out. He wanted to get an advantage over Evelyn. He needed that. He needed her properly afraid of him or she would never help him. She was the only one who could, much as he hated that notion. Her or one of her flunkies, one of them somewhere had to know how to get rid of his Other. He needed that freedom.

Chapter Thirty-One

Not-Tina

SOLE DEMARCO HANDED OVER the weapons without any trouble at all, especially after she waved the money under his nose. He wasn't smart, but he was greedy and that made her happy. After that, Not-Tina felt a little better about the way her day was going.

Fun fact she did not expect: lots of people put their phone numbers out for the public to see. Josh Warburton was one of them. He was actually that stupid. It wasn't the phone number that was the problem for him, though; it was the address. She found his home with remarkable ease, and then she stowed a few weapons at a house about a block away.

A casual stroll through the neighborhood told her most of what she needed to know. First, she got a good whiff of the man's house and realized that several people lived there. Judging by the toys in the front and back yards, he had at least two kids. She also saw the maid service go in, so she got to see his wife answer the door. Nice place. Tina could have fit around ten of her last apartments in there.

She also got a good idea of what the man smelled like. Maybe not quite good enough to track him from his house to work, unfortunately, but definitely good enough to recognize him when he came home. That was the best part about scents: they lingered like fingerprints. If Warburton walked to work, she could have followed him. He took a car, and the smells from his car weren't distinct enough for her to separate out from all the other vehicles on the road. Maybe given enough time, but she hadn't really had much practice at any of this yet, and she was winging it.

So instead she waited, patient as could be, for Warburton to come home. Meanwhile, she needed to take care of other matters.

She was starting a war. That takes time and effort. The money she'd used earlier was earmarked for costs and expenses while she was in town, hotel rooms and travel and all sorts of other things, but while that mattered to Joe and she liked Joe, it wasn't the only priority in Not-Tina's mind. She had vendettas of her own to handle. Scarabelli and his lieutenants came immediately to mind.

While she sat in the bushes of the house closest to Warburton's place, she contemplated the issues she had to get boiling a little faster if she wanted her plans to work.

Sol DeMarco liked to talk when he was working. He liked to brag, especially to pretty girls. Maybe Not-Tina wasn't as fine as Kyrie or her counterpart, but she had been good enough to keep Sol's attention all on her own. She had listened while he bragged, and she had flirted and made sure that he knew how impressed she was by all of his connections. And like all men who like to brag, he had dropped names.

The cell phone in her back pocket worked just fine. She dialed the number from memory as she leaned against the brick wall in the upscale neighborhood. School had let out, and kids her own age walked past, most of them lost in the drama of their own lives, not the least bit interested in the chaos she was brewing. Maybe if it got made into a movie, they'd care. Either way, they barely mattered to her, except for the blond boy who walked past. He was damned cute. She bet she could put a smile on his face.

Instead she listened until the fourth ring, and when Scarabelli's voice told her to leave a message, she did. "You know who this is," she purred into the phone. "I just wanted to let you know I got some help to take care of you. Niko Belucci sends his love. Says when I see you, I should remind you about his cousin and that little thing that was supposed to happen that didn't." She paused for a moment and closed her eyes, imagining his fat face as he heard the words. "I'm coming for you, piggy. You're gonna be squealing soon.

You're gonna bleed."

She hung up the phone and smiled, knowing he was going to go nuts when he heard her words. He was also going to get himself into a lot of trouble with one of Chicago's meanest dogs. She liked to think about how that would play out. She could almost imagine him going into one of his rants. His little fits amused her.

The warm glow she got from thinking about Scarabelli all pissed off kept her comfy and cozy for the next two hours while she waited for her target to finally come home. She still waited, settling back and staring through the hedges next to the house.

There were things she still had to consider.

And she was waiting for her orders.

What's my name? The thought came to her unbidden, and she craned her head around to make sure no one had snuck up close to her. Not-Tina wasn't so much a name as a way to separate her from the screaming little crybaby locked inside her at the moment. She knew that. She should have come up with a name before then, but she had been busy with other things, more important things, like the tattoo on her arm and pissing off the mobsters that had offended her by being alive.

A flutter of fear ran through her. The feeling was mostly a ghost, a little leftover emotion from Tina, but this time it was real and that meant she had to consider it. If she was afraid, there had to be a reason.

Not-Tina shook that away. No. She didn't do fear. She didn't like to be afraid. That was Tina's way. She was afraid of having a name? Forget that!

"Theresa. That's my name." It was just that simple. She spoke her name and that ghost of fear went away. Of course she knew what it was. Commitment. Having a name was something permanent, and she didn't like things that were forever. She liked things to change, give or take the occasional tattoo. That was the other difference between her and Tina. Tina wanted everything to be calm and stable, and Theresa didn't like that at all. She liked things to be crazy.

She let herself smile a bit and was about to find a different hiding place when the man she'd been waiting on came home.

He never made it to the front door.

Theresa slid out of the hedges in a low crouch and looked Josh Warburton over. He was a little butterball of a man, but she knew a guy didn't have to be all muscles and guns to have power. Scarabelli had taught her that. That fat old bastard had ruined Tina's father and mother without ever touching them. He had that kind of power. So did Warburton.

Josh Warburton probably never touched Tina in his life—or Theresa for that matter—but he was responsible for what they were, same as Evelyn Hope. He had people that worked for him. He had power.

Theresa envied that. So she was more than glad to take it from him.

Before he could scream, Theresa had her hand over his mouth and was pulling him to the side of his house. She'd looked the place over carefully. This spot, on the right side of the house, just under the start of the back porch, was dark and secluded, and the neighbors didn't have windows that looked down on it.

Warburton grunted and fought, his hands punching and clawing at her even as she dragged his little piggy self around the side of the house, an enormous structure that he probably thought of as his castle. Theresa pushed him down into the dirt and debris under the porch, into the shadows where he hid the imperfect parts of his world, cast-off gardening gloves and a hose that had seen better days along with a few of his kids' toys that had long since lost their appeal.

He deserved to see the darker parts of his life a little better. Theresa was glad to be the one to show him.

He was a grown man and he was strong for his size, but he wasn't physically created to be a killer. She was. When he looked into her face for a moment, she knew he recognized her for what she was too. Maybe there was something about studying the subjects they'd killed that let the fat man understand what made her different. Maybe he was just realizing that she'd kill him as soon as look at him. Either way was okay with Theresa. Either way he finally calmed down, panting heavily against the hand that covered his mouth.

"You Josh?" She leaned in closer and looked into his eyes. He was thinking about lying. She could tell by the way he didn't quite look into her eyes. "Before you answer, I've already looked inside, seen the wife, the kids, the maid. I'll kill them all if you lie to me. Don't think I'm kidding. I've killed worse for less." That wasn't quite true, but it was close.

He nodded and sighed against her palm and fingers. She nodded in return and spoke softly. "This is between you and me. No one else has to be involved. But if you scream or get stupid, I'll make you watch while I kill 'em."

She leaned in even closer, her body hovering over his in a way that some would have found compromising, though she knew neither of them were even close to feeling frisky in that way. "Here's the thing. You and your people, you made me and mine. You took my friends away. All of them. I want them back." She took her hand away from his mouth so she could see his face.

"What do you want me to do?"

"You're going to tell me where they are. And then you're going to help me get to them."

"I can't do that." His voice was trembling a bit, but he was good at trying to hide it.

Her hand covered his mouth again, tightly.

Theresa leaned in until her lips were against his ear. "Don't scream, or I'll kill your family." The words were whispered as softly as a baby's breath.

Theresa caught his hand in hers and sought just one digit. The sound of his little finger breaking was only a little louder than her voice had been.

Warburton gasped, and despite her warning, the pain made him scream. He bucked and thrashed and she pinned him in place, smiling at his discomfort. Even at her worst, Tina would have felt bad for the man. Theresa just enjoyed the show.

"That was one. Give me three screams, they all die. Not kidding around here. Mean it." She kept her voice low, and even when he tried to roll over and get away, she held her lips close to his ear and kept him pinned in place.

Her eyes looked him over and the expression on her face told exactly how little she thought of what she was seeing. "You think you're so damned tough. So smart and so rich. You aren't anything that I can't get rid of, Josh. You get me?" Her voice was pure venom and hatred, and she let that much show without hesitation. She wanted him to know exactly how much she could ruin him.

"I only dislocated one little joint. You're smart. You

can tell all your friends how you closed your finger in the car door, and everyone will believe you. Trust me, this is nothing. I can do a lot worse, stuff you can't begin to hide." She sniffed. He stank of fear and pain.

She let her hand leave his mouth again.

"I have money." He wanted to bargain.

"So do I. If I want more, I'll get it. What I want from you is my friends." She looked into his eyes. He was scared, but not scared enough. Not yet.

"What am I supposed to do?" he asked again.

Theresa smiled and leaned in so close she could have kissed him if she wanted. She most definitely did not want that. "You know what I am?"

"A Doppelganger."

"No. A Failure. You and yours, you threw me out with the dishwater. I'm supposed to be dead. So, really, I ain't got a lot to lose here." She smiled to make her point. "And what little I have, you just took away from me. Those other Failures, see, they're all I've got left. You took my family. I want it back." She covered his hand again and found a second finger, and though he wanted to fight, he didn't dare. "Or I take from you. I take everything. I kill that pretty family. I break your legs. I break your hands. I break out your teeth and leave you to find them and collect them with your broken fingers. You getting me here?"

He nodded vigorously. "Yes. Got you." She smiled and

released his finger, unbroken this time.

"Tell me where my family is. You tell me where the others you took from me are, Josh Warburton, or I. Will. Destroy. You."

She sat up and moved off of him, letting him slowly sit up. His eyes were wide now, fearful. There might have been a little craftiness hiding in there before, but it was difficult to detect if it was still there.

"What do you want from me?"

"You need to do everything you can to make sure my family is safe so that your family can be safe."

The two of them left the shadows under his house and moved toward his car together.

Chapter Thirty-Two

Kyrie Merriwether/Not-Kyrie

KYRIE LOOKED AT HANK with concern. He was sweating so much that he'd soaked through the simple jumpsuit he wore. The garment had been fitted to Cody, and the difference in their sizes left the fabric strained and taut across his body. His face was turned away from her at first, but eventually he looked toward her with eyes that saw nothing at all. He didn't focus on her; he merely aimed his eyes in her general direction.

Gene coughed and sighed. "We're never getting out of here."

"Can you not be so negative? We don't even know what's going on, not really."

"You think so?" Gene laughed, but it wasn't an amused sound. "You think they're going to let us go? They're going to either cut us open and see what makes us tick, or they're just going to kill us. You heard the others. We shouldn't even exist."

It was Hank that answered, before Kyrie could come up with a proper response. "We'll get out. I have a plan."

Gene laughed again and Kyrie hated him right then, because even his laugh sounded bitter and angry. "You have a plan? Well, I feel all reassured now, brother."

"You *are* my brother. You get that, right? You are my brother." Hank's voice sounded strangely soft and almost tender, which was unusual for him. "I never had a brother before, Gene. I want to keep you now that I have you."

Gene's face grew slack for a second as he considered the words. Then he closed his mouth, uncertain how to respond.

Kyrie turned her head away. She had brothers and sisters and a mother and a father and she wanted to get back to them. Her heart pounded in her chest and she bit her lip to avoid making a noise. Homesickness washed over her like a tidal wave.

And as the wave of longing drew back, the darkness came for her as it had again and again since the first time she heard Joe call out to wake up the thing that hid inside her.

Not-Kyrie was waking up, and Kyrie was too tired to care, too tired to stop her. *Let her come. Maybe she can fix all of this.*

And a moment later, Kyrie was gone.

Not-Kyrie opened her eyes and looked around, examining

the restraints that held her, turning toward Gene where he lay strapped in place, staring at her with wide eyes. Cute kid, but a coward through and through. She didn't much like him. Cute didn't mean a thing if he didn't have the guts to live his life.

"What the hell are you staring at?" She couldn't keep the contempt out of her voice.

Gene flinched as surely as if she'd slapped him.

Hank cleared his throat and she looked his way, shocked by how pale he was, how drenched in his own perspiration.

"He's looking at you," Hank told her. "He's freaked out because he just watched you change for the first time. Takes a little getting used to."

Not-Kyrie stared at him for a long moment, but before she could think of anything to say, the oversized brute closed his eyes and drifted into a feverish slumber.

She looked away from him and back toward Gene. He was looking at his reflection in the mirror that faced them all, his lips pressed together into an angry slit. His chest heaved with each deep breath he took and she thought for a moment that he would surely break into tears. The very idea filled her with contempt. Boys were supposed to be stronger than girls, and here he was, ready to cry like a baby.

No. Her bad. He wasn't about to cry, he was about to change. She stared as his body grew rigid.

"No. Don't want this." His voice was strained and his

eyes grew wide and very frightened. "Let me stay."

Gene's body thrashed hard against the restraints and Not-Kyrie watched, excited. She wanted to know this, to see this, to understand what happened to her own body when the change came around. Gene's muscles shifted fluidly, growing larger all at once, swelling as the bones beneath them expanded in length and thickness both. His hair grew longer, his face broadened, his skin became two shades darker, as if he'd been tanning at the pool for a couple of days.

On one side of her, Hank looked almost as oversized as a shaved gorilla, massive and distorted. In comparison to that, Sam seemed almost tiny but still much larger than Gene had been. He grew a full six inches in height and easily as much in width. He changed. That was all there was to it. When he was Gene, he looked like a fifteen-year-old boy. When he was Sam, he looked like a fifteen-year-old boy who'd spent his entire life working out hard and heavy on a daily basis. He was bigger, harder, more *vital.* Gene could be ignored. Sam could not.

Sam looked at her for a moment, then at the restraints on his wrists and ankles. He grunted once, then started thrashing, pulling and twisting in an effort to get free from his bonds.

"Who the hell did this?" His words were a demand for knowledge, not merely a question.

He got nowhere with his restraints, and rather than answer him, she decided to show him how it was done. Not-Kyrie slammed her body forward and back in an effort to get away from her examination table, with absolutely no luck.

Next to her, Hank let out a low moan and slumped back into a fitful sleep.

Not-Kyrie let out a scream of frustration. This, this was not what she wanted from the world, and she was so tired of being patient. She wanted to be free once and for all, like Joe had promised. Instead she was held captive more than ever before.

Someone would pay dearly.

Chapter Thirty-Three

Cody Laurel

THE FEVER DISTORTED EVERYTHING. Cody felt his skin shiver, his muscles twitch.

What's happening to me? He asked the question only to himself.

Us. What's happening to us. Hank's voice answered him. At least he thought it was Hank's. They hadn't really met before.

Whatever. What's happening?

We're dying.

I don't want to die.

Neither do I, Hank replied.

I was kind of looking forward to getting to know you. I was hoping we could be friends.

Me too. I don't need enemies in my life. There are enough of those already, aren't there?

Yeah. It was weird to think that the two of them could talk, and maybe they weren't as different as he'd expected. *Say, did you break Hank Chadbourne's arm and Glenn Wagner's wrist?*

Of course.

Why?

They were douches. They needed to be taught a lesson.

Well, thanks then. I mean it.

It's all good, man.

He couldn't think of anything to say after that, and he felt the pain again, a rolling agony that twisted flesh and meat and bone and nerves into new shapes that danced with tortured strain.

On the other hand, I don't know if I can take this much longer. My heart—our heart—feels like it's gonna explode. Hank's voice was much more rational than he'd actually expected.

So what do we do about it?

There was a long silence.

I guess we need to work together.

How?

Well, that's the challenge, isn't it? We aren't designed for this.

They were both quiet for a while.

Finally, Hank spoke to him again. *I think I have an idea.*

Well, don't keep me in suspense here.

On the examination table their shared body bucked and shivered, and their teeth gnashed down and shredded their lips as their body seized and twitched, oblivious to the two other forms in the room.

And then the most glorious thing happened . . .

Chapter Thirty-Four

Joe Bronx

JOE OPENED HIS EYES after resting as best he could in the restraints. His body was sore. He felt the needles that pumped drugs into his body and had to hold back his desire to howl his anger to the universe.

Anger was a tool, and losing his temper for no purpose achieved exactly nothing. Still, he wanted to rage.

He looked at the heavy bonds on his wrists and shook his head. Surely they were strong enough to hold him. Surely they had been made for that exact reason. Bobby's mother would never make a mistake about a thing like that, would she?

Of course, he'd broken free before, hadn't he?

Joe calmed his breathing and stared at his reflection. Maybe it was true that he was a monster. Maybe he was a vicious killer, and he knew full well that Evelyn thought it of him. Maybe he was all of that and more, but all he saw in the reflective wall was the same thing he always saw—the hero of the story.

His story.

No one else mattered, not really. He was the only one who meant anything when you got right down to it. It was probably that way for everyone, wasn't it? Why would anyone want to be the sidekick in their own lives?

And if he was the hero of his story, he would have to come to his own rescue.

He forced his body to relax, then focused on his right arm, slowly, carefully straining against the cuff that pinned his wrist in place. He could feel the muscles in his forearm clenching and pulling, could feel where the cuff cut into his skin despite the attempted protection offered by the heavy padding.

Bones groaned beneath his flesh, and the table he rested on made a soft noise of protest.

He did not make a sound, but merely breathed softly again as he continued to focus his strength. In the long run, it came down to a simple matter: Who was stronger?

"I am."

He spoke with absolute conviction. Nothing would stop him.

Nothing.

His brow was covered with sweat and his muscles

shook—shivered—still, he pushed himself. Still he strained with just the one arm against the cuff that held him.

The bones beneath his flesh groaned, and so did the table he pulled against.

One of them would give. It was just a question of which one.

Joe's teeth ground together and his jaw clenched against the growing pain in his arm. The bones were not meant to withstand this sort of pressure. He was beginning to think he understood his own limitations.

"No. Screw that. No limits, you little wimp." He mumbled the words, but spoke them with venom just the same. He would not fail, not now. Not ever.

Something hot flared and popped in his wrist. The pain was like a lightning bolt through his nervous system.

Several profanities escaped his lips and he pulled all the harder. Beneath him, the table let out a groan of pain that matched his own and Joe pulled harder still, every muscle in his arm strained and his entire torso reddened by the blood that wanted to move into his muscles and give him extra strength.

"Not going to let you win, you bitch." The words weren't for him this time. They were for Evelyn. How had he thought he could ever reason with her? How could he have believed for even a second that she was rational and would help him get free from the son she loved and missed?

The son she loved, while she hated him.

Anger fueled him, fed the burning hatred that he was using for motivation.

Anger was a tool.

He knew how to use the tools at his disposal.

The next sound wasn't of something threatening to break. It was the sound of something shattering.

Chapter Thirty-Five

Evelyn Hope

EVELYN WAS IN JOSH'S office when George found her. She needed to get her work done, and that meant she needed a computer. The only person in the company with the same clearance as her was Josh, so she took over when he went home for the day.

George cleared his throat and waited for her to acknowledge him. That was wise. She was already in a mood.

"Spill it, George. What's wrong?" She didn't bother looking up from the screen and her fingers kept typing.

"Subject Seven is trying to break free."

She looked at George over the edge of the computer monitor. "That's like telling me that the newborn baby pooped his diapers. Did he escape?"

"No. But he's working very hard at it."

"Have him sedated again."

George nodded, but stayed where he was.

"What else, George?"

"The others that were with him have all changed. They've gone into their aggressive modes." George tried to keep up with the jargon, but inevitably failed.

"They're called Doppelgangers, George."

"They're big and mean and they've all changed. Beyond that, I know nothing."

"Fair enough. See about having them all sedated. We don't want any incidents."

He nodded and headed back toward the hallway. She almost called him back but changed her mind at the last moment. She needed time to think, to be alone with her memories and her anxieties.

She needed time to be just a little afraid.

Then she'd go about making everything all right. She'd see to Gabby and Bobby and—

No. Evelyn's lips pressed together and she shook her head. She couldn't allow herself to think like that. Bobby wasn't back. Not yet and maybe not ever. That was what she had to figure out, wasn't it?

Could she keep her son and get rid of the monster inside of him? She didn't know, but she'd find out. If there was any chance at all, she'd take it.

And if there wasn't any chance, then she had to be ready

for that too, didn't she? There might not be a way to fix this. There might not be any way at all to have her son back without Seven coming along for the ride. If Subject Seven was a part of the equation—if he was a permanent fixture—she'd have to kill him. That was all there was to it. He was too dangerous.

The computer screen in front of her broke apart, fractured into a million flares of light as tears started forming in her eyes.

"No. Absolutely not." She angrily wiped the tears away. She'd said her goodbyes to Bobby a long time ago. She kept his memories alive in her heart, but that didn't mean she had to have him alive and with her any more than she had to have Tom back in her life.

If Bobby could not be kept alive without Subject Seven, then she would accept that her son was dead. It was the way the world had to be. There had to be reason before everything else, especially when it came to Seven. He was a monster. He was too dangerous to be left intact.

She'd have to let someone else perform the autopsy, of course. She wasn't quite strong enough to handle that part herself, not this time. She'd handled the autopsies in the past, but none of them had been her son. None of them had been the one she adopted into her life. Not one of them had been Bobby.

Still, there was always a possibility, wasn't there? That

was why she was looking over all of the notes herself and double checking all of the figures on the blood tests and the examinations of both Seven's skull and Bobby's.

One last chance to have her son back. Or one final chance to have revenge on the nightmare that killed her husband and stole her son once and for all. She'd have one or the other. She had earned that much satisfaction from the world, even if the world did not completely agree with her on the subject.

Chapter Thirty-Six

Theresa

"YOU REALLY DON'T GET it, do you?" Theresa spoke and Warburton listened, but only because he was a captive audience. "See, you think this is all about your little soldiers. But me? I think it's all about what I want. The difference is, your soldiers aren't here and I am, so I guess that makes me right and you wrong." Warburton looked her way for a moment and tried to repress a shiver.

He was scared, not least because she'd never driven a car before and her skills left a bit to be desired. The lanes didn't seem nearly as wide when she was behind the wheel. She wasn't scared. She knew she wasn't going to wreck. On the other hand, it wasn't her expensive car she was driving, either.

"Tell me when to turn," she said.

"There's absolutely no way you can break into the

compound without being stopped." He was no fun at all.

"You keep sayin' that, and I keep thinking you're wrong, and we're not gonna agree on this one, tubs, so you might as well just tell me where to turn."

"I didn't say I wouldn't tell you; I'm just trying to warn you."

"Consider me warned. Keep on telling me, though, because I'm still just fine with killing the wife and the kids."

He clammed up and pointed to the right at the next intersection.

She turned and slowed down as the road rolled into a large parking lot. "See? That wasn't so rough." Her words trailed off as she looked around. "So, where's this compound?"

When he didn't answer, Theresa turned to face him and got a brutal elbow to her face. Her head snapped back and the man struck her again and again and a fourth time, sending the back of her head into the tempered glass on the driver's side. Her nose took a hard strike and started bleeding. Her lips got mashed hard into her teeth.

As Josh Warburton was reaching to hit her once more, Theresa kicked him in his chest and took all the fight out of him.

She angled the rearview mirror to look at her face and saw the spots where her skin was already busted or swelling. Then she looked back at the moron who'd tried to hurt her.

Warburton was gasping, his arms wrapped around his

stomach as he doubled over and moaned.

Theresa caught his face in her hand and pulled him across the seat until he was close to her. “How damn stupid are you?” She pushed him backward until his head smacked against the window. She didn’t speak—she screamed at him, her face reddened by anger and blood-tainted spittle spraying from her busted lips. “I’ll find the place one way or another. You keep making me look, I’ll find it without you. If I find it without you, it’ll be because you’re dead and your family is dead, do you get me?”

He didn’t answer. He was too busy trying to breathe.

But the voice inside her skull was clear. *Don’t kill him. He might have pass codes or a security key that you’ll need.*

She frowned. The voice wasn’t what she expected. It wasn’t Joe’s. She was sure of that now. Still, it made sense to listen to this one too. Because it was . . . well, because it was right.

Warburton opened his mouth to say something again and Theresa shook her finger. “Just keep your fat mouth shut. Only thing I wanna hear from you is driving directions.”

He stared at her for a long moment, and she could see him playing it over again in his head. He’d hit her hard four times, and she was barely fazed. She’d kicked him once and had probably broken a rib or two.

He finally pointed in the direction they’d come from. Before she started driving, she spat blood on the car floor and glared at him. "Last chance, little piggy. You do me wrong again, I'll kill all of them. Your family, your friends and then you."

Twenty minutes passed with little more than an occasional gesture between them before he finally directed her to a medical center not far from the local hospital.

She parked the car and took the keys from the ignition, sliding them into her jeans pocket. "Get out of the car. You're coming with."

"I won't help you get in there." He shook his head.

"Two choices. We go in. Or I go say hi to the wifey." She opened the truck and pulled out her bag of goodies. Considering how much she'd paid, it didn't seem like much.

Then again, sometimes big things came in small packages. At least, that was what Tina's mom always said—before she wound up dead in the river.

Josh was looking at her stash, and she could almost see the gears in his head working on whether or not he could get the contents away from her.

"You even think too hard about what I'm carrying, and I'll break both of your thumbs." Theresa looked him up and down again, a scowl showing how little she thought of his chances. "Can't do much of anything without them. Saw a kid try all summer long, but she couldn't even hold her own sodas. So you get to feeling like trying your luck without thumbs, you go for it. Otherwise, look somewhere else. You're too old to be giving me the eye like that." He hadn't been, but she liked the look of discomfort he got on his face.

Theresa set her hand on his shoulder and gave a squeeze hard enough to make him wince. "Lead the way. You set off any alarms, I'll kill you before anything can happen to me. You believe me?"

Before he could answer, the first sirens went off.

Chapter Thirty-Seven

Sam Hall

SAM STRAINED AGAINST HIS bonds again, his anger growing like a forest fire: one little spark that was rapidly getting hungrier and hungrier.

This wasn't the plan. He'd told Evelyn Hope the exact time, given her every advantage, sold out the others for a chance at a real life. He knew there was a possibility of betrayal, but he'd been hoping hard that he could get away with it. Now that he had realized he wasn't going to get free of the situation or the tiresome Other hiding inside of him, the smoldering little flame had become a conflagration.

Calm down. The thought came into his head without warning, and before he even realized it, he was actually obeying, relaxing against his bonds.

"What?" The sound of his own voice surprised him.

Calm down. They're coming. We're going to get you out of there.

"Who are you?" He looked around the small room. Not-Kyrie was looking around, puzzled as he was, but other than that there wasn't much to see.

"Is there a voice in your head?" He asked the question of Not-Kyrie, who looked back and nodded, making him feel just that little bit better about himself. Maybe he wasn't going insane. He'd accepted that Joe could talk in his head, but that was the only voice he'd ever heard there until now.

"And it isn't Joe?"

"No."

Shut the hell up. I'm concentrating. I have to time this just right and after that it's up to the two of you.

"All right. Who the hell is that?"

Cody/Hank growled. "Who do you think it is, dumb ass? Now shut up for a minute."

Sam was about to tell Hank where he could shove his attitude when the other boy groaned again and grew smaller. That was the only way to put it. He deflated down to Cody's size and shivered violently. As he was letting out a moan, he slid his hands free of their restraints. Both of his wrists were hideously bruised, almost black, but he ignored them and reached for his ankles.

"Damn it, still too tight." The voice was wrong, too weak to even be Cody's, and the runt was already high and squeaky. Just the same, Sam saw the boy grab the leg restraint in thin fingers and slip his hands completely around the thick metal before he changed again, growing almost violently. The skin on his body was slippery with sweat, and there were several angry-looking red marks around his joints. Sam had never seen them firsthand, but Gene had. They looked like the stretch marks on Gene's mother's waist when she was pregnant with Trish. The skin had grown too much, and rather than rupture, it stretched. Hank was covered with stretch marks much the same way, but in different areas.

Hank let out a low groan, and his arms trembled as he grabbed the metal cuff and pulled. Sam thought for sure that he would give up, but instead the metal let out a wounded shriek and split along the seam. Hank's right leg was freed.

He hopped off the table, his left leg still stuck in the same position as before. He reached out and grabbed again, his fingernails pulling the fabric of the jumpsuit roughly out of his way.

Tell me when you hear they're almost here. The mental voice was calm and almost confusing when compared to the wounded, angry sounds coming from Hank/Cody's mouth. His body was still changing, not quite settling into any particular size.

Sam had no idea what the hell he was talking about.

"I can hear them talking. They're almost at the door." Not-Kyrie spoke, her voice tense, her face showing her anxiety. She actually thought that Hank was going to get them out of this.

Hank grunted again and the sound of metal snapping gave away the fact that he'd freed himself. Sam had tried—and hard—to work the restraints free, but to no avail. Hank had just freed himself and Sam had failed. That didn't sit well.

Rather than speaking to either of them, Hank moved his bulk against the wall near the door, where he would be hardest to see when whoever was coming showed up.

His blood stained the torn fabric on the left leg of his jumper. Whatever he'd done to free himself, he'd been injured in the process.

Not-Kyrie suddenly threw herself against her restraints, screaming loud enough to deafen. "Let me out of here, you bastards!" She was glaring at the door even as it opened. Sam had not heard anything as they came closer, but somehow Not-Kyrie had known.

Two men entered the room, and a third was in the hallway beyond them. Sam could see that much.

"You need to calm down." The man speaking had a deep voice and a southern drawl. He shaved his head and probably thought he looked intimidating, but Sam thought he looked a little too melon-like to be tough.

The gun in his hand, however, was a different story. It wasn't killing weapon, but a dart gun. Whatever was in the darts would probably be very strong.

"Bite me, loser!" Not-Kyrie was keeping it up, throwing herself toward them with all of her strength. Her body strained and fell back, arched and slumped, making him think of a dog straining against a leash.

The man took two steps forward and aimed the gun at her midriff.

Hank's hand closed over his hand and the gun and squeezed. Baldy's eyes flew wide, and he let out a yelp that quickly became a scream as the bones in his hand cracked and broke, making a sound like muffled firecrackers.

He thrashed and tried to escape from the overwhelming pain, but he failed. Hank pulled the man the rest of the way into the room and threw him aside. Then he reached into the hallway and grabbed at the remaining men.

They were quick to retreat.

But Hank was faster. He didn't speak or make light of the situation for once. When they'd had to take on a bar full of bikers, Hank had been cheerfully violent, laughing and making smart-ass comments as he fought. That was gone now, replaced by the sweating, bloodied, straining giant who battered both of his victims into unconsciousness without a word.

Sam tried to watch the violence—to see what the hell was going on—but the angle was wrong. Not-Kyrie watched, however, a smile growing on her face.

"He got the keys."

A moment later, Hank staggered back into the room, his hands shaking and covered in blood. He was holding a small ring of keys. He didn't bother looking at Sam. Instead he unlocked the restraints holding Not-Kyrie.

"What about me?"

Hank looked toward him, his eyes dark with menace. When he spoke, it was internal, with his mind. Sam could see that Not-Kyrie heard nothing of the words.

What about you? You sold us out. I read it in your mind. You told them where we would be and when we'd get there. You let them know we had weapons and that we'd be showing up on the bikes. I should leave you to die, you little bitch.

Anger and shame mingled in Sam's innards and he felt his face blush red at the same time that his stomach froze with dread.

"I-"

Don't say it out loud. No one else knows. Let's keep it that way.

Without saying another word, Hank moved over and unlocked his wrists quickly. While he went to work on Sam's ankles, Not-Kyrie moved. She shook her wrists and legs, working blood back into areas that hadn't gotten enough to stay comfortable.

Hank stepped back. *You're free. You want to help me,*

stay with us. You want to run off and save yourself, do it now. But if you ever betray us again, Sam, I'll kill you.

Sam trembled. Hank wasn't going to leave him to die or even tell anyone else. He was giving Sam a choice, something that had never really been offered before.

"I'll help." The words crept out of his mouth like secrets.

Hank nodded and said, "Good." Then he fell on his face and shrank in size, reverting to Cody.

Not-Kyrie looked at Cody for a few seconds, then grabbed him, lifting his weight with ease and draping him over her shoulder. She was a good deal smaller than Sam, but she was strong.

"You gonna stare at me all day? Or are we getting the hell out of here?" Her voice caught him off guard. He'd been lost in the strange mix of guilt and anger. He had to work on that.

And he'd have to work fast. The alarms sounded as they entered the hallway. Someone knew they'd gotten free.

Chapter Thirty-Eight

Joe Bronx

THE BELLS STARTED RINGING before he even tried to make a break for it. Joe suppressed a smile. This was better than he'd hoped. The alarm meant that some of the guards would be distracted, and maybe, if he was very lucky, some of his friends had escaped already.

When the guards came by to check on him, Joe behaved himself and slumped back against his table. They were scared of him. He needed to make sure they weren't scared enough to shoot. Not yet, at least.

There were cameras, of course. They could see it when he was struggling to break free. They could hear him when he cursed under his breath, and every time he got too busy with the struggling to break free, they came back into the room again.

He needed to make sure that stopped because he was finally ready to get the hell out of the room.

He'd almost shattered the bones in his wrist earlier, but in the long run he'd managed to break the restraint instead. He'd almost let that fact slip at first, but he'd covered it over by screaming for Evelyn to come tuck him into his bed. She was out there somewhere and probably close by. He knew it, could sense it, and knew her well enough to know that she would never leave her precious boy Bobby alone, not when he was so near.

Had she figured out what Subject Seven had discovered a long time ago? Yes, she had. Bobby was coming back. He'd been gone for almost five years after the car hit Joe in the head. Whatever brain cells made up Bobby had been damaged, crushed by the blow. Now they were coming back. Bobby was coming back. Hunter was bad enough, but Bobby? That little worm would try to run home to his mommy at every opportunity. The thought was enough to make Joe grind his teeth.

This had to end. He'd find a way.

But first there was the matter of getting free.

He worked his arms first and then his legs. The restraints gave easily now. Enough force and you could bend almost anything. He didn't need to break the bonds, only to stretch them. And he had.

The guards would come soon. Very soon. He could hear their heartbeats. They were nice and steady. Good. Earlier they had been worried, afraid the restraints wouldn't hold, perhaps, or that the big scary monster man might shoot lasers from his eyes. He didn't know for sure what they'd been thinking—only that they had been very cautious and more than a little scared. Now routine was making them cocky. He hadn't misbehaved nearly enough, and that meant he was safe and secure in his room.

He could have broken out at any point in the last hour, but that wouldn't have worked for him.

First he needed the guards to be complacent, because they had weapons, and he wanted those weapons for his own.

Closer. They were coming closer. Seven made himself relax.

Five steps away.

Four. Three. Two. One.

The door opened, letting in the sound of the alarm bells going loud and proud.

And Joe leaped.

Chapter Thirty-Nine

Theresa

WARBURTON BACKED UP, HIS hands held high above his head. "I didn't do anything! You see me! I didn't do anything!" He was afraid she'd kill him. That made him smarter than he looked, because she was seriously considering it.

Stay calm. You can't lose it. If you go crazy now, everyone dies.

Theresa listened to the voice, nodded to herself and pointed the business end of her .357 Magnum at Warburton's round, nervous face.

"Shut it. Start walking. Any security problems, you fix them or I fix you." She slipped away into the shadows, leaving the man looking around desperately before he finally decided he should do as he was told.

The man walked around to the side of the building and

went to a security keypad that required both a code and a card key. She watched him carefully as he entered in his code and ran the magnetic stripe on the card. Then as the door in front of him opened, she moved fast, urging him through the door and slipping in with him.

Her eyes were far more sensitive than his, so she saw the way he licked his lips and the way his eyes moved to the left. Nervous signs. "Tells" is what Tony Parmiatto called them. Signs that someone knew something more than he should have and was nervous about it. Tina had doted on every word Tony said. That was good, because all the little things he told her were making Theresa's life a lot easier. Theresa slid to the right, crouching low and moving behind Warburton's stocky body. He wasn't tall, but he made a great shield. When she looked around his shoulder, she saw the camera's small red light. Security. She could handle security. She'd half expected a guard with a gun.

As they moved out of the room and down a small corridor she eyeballed the walls and ceiling, looking for more cameras. Nothing made itself known to her.

Warburton's face kissed the wall roughly as she pushed him against it and slid the barrel of her weapon against the side of his neck. "Skip telling me about any other cameras or security. Please," she dared him. "I promise the first shot will just blow out your arm, or maybe your leg." She leaned in close until she was once again violating his personal space and pushing his whole body against the wall. "You believe me? You want me to prove it?"

He whined. "No. Please. I'm sorry. I got scared is all."

"Don't get scared and you don't get dead. Just get me to where my friends are, or I kill you. It's that easy."

She resisted the urgc to slap the back of his head for his trouble. The hallway led to one doorway and nothing else. She grabbed his shoulder and pushed him in front of her. If a bullet was coming for someone, it was going to have his name on it, not hers.

The doorway opened into an empty room. On the other side of the small room was an elevator. "Okay, seriously, do you guys have a lot of these places around?"

"What do you mean?"

"A door to a hallway to a room that leads to an elevator. Is there really a place here? Or are you screwing with me?"

"We don't exactly have our offices out in the open." He shook his head. "We deal in genetically altered mercenaries and high-tech weapons. You can't just sell what we sell at the local strip mall."

"Just get us where we're going before I get bored." The sad part was she was serious. She was getting bored, and if she got too tired of waiting around, there was a chance that Tina would want out. She couldn't have that. Not yet.

Warburton reached into his pocket—carefully when she slid the weapon against his neck again—and found the key ring that let him activate the elevator.

"What's with the alarms, anyway?"

"For all I know someone just tried to break into one of the real clinics." He shrugged, but his pulse rate spiked. He was lying. She didn't call him on it, not this time.

"Your life. Your choices to make. I'm just sayin' is all."

Warburton licked his lips. "Maybe it's us. Maybe one of your friends tried to get away." She tried to focus, but she couldn't feel Joe's presence in her head. The other one was there, though, weak but there.

Can you tell me what's going on? Theresa thought. She wasn't sure if she could communicate with the new voice unless it talked first, but she had to try.

No. I'm not sure. There are people all around, moving, running, but I don't know why. The voice was distorted, fading in and out.

Who is this?

There was no answer. Instead a loud bell rang and the elevator doors opened. Warburton started forward and Theresa grabbed him. "There a camera?"

He nodded, not quite daring to speak.

"Where?"

"Front of the car, on the left side."

She let him move into the elevator and slipped in herself, crouching low as she moved under the position he claimed had the camera. Maybe it would see her. Maybe it wouldn't.

That was the best she could do.

As the car started descending, the sound of alarms grew louder and louder. Warburton looked at her and then looked away, moving from foot to foot nervously.

"Calm down. You stay calm, no one has to get hurt."

He swallowed hard. "It might be too late for that."

Before she could ask him what he meant, the car came to a soft stop.

Theresa tapped the pistol softly against her leg, careful to leave the barrel pointed away from her. It wouldn't do her any good to blow her leg off.

When the door opened, she didn't wait. She moved, pushing past the sliding metal and checking the hallway around her. There was nothing to see except another small room, almost identical to the one she'd left when she got in the elevator. The difference was that there was a security desk at this one. It was empty.

She grabbed Warburton just as he was reaching for the elevator buttons, apparently to try to maybe close the door and get the hell out of there.

"How many warnings I got to give you before you decide I'm serious!?" The alarms were louder down here, so she let herself yell as she pulled him in closer, pushing him against the wall. "You want to piss me off? You want to bleed?"

He winced as she pushed the weapon against his leg. "No! I'm sorry! I'm just scared!"

"Be scared! But be smart! I swear to God I should just kill your sad ass right now!"

Warburton closed his eyes and trembled, and Theresa smiled to herself. It was nice to be in charge. She could get used to it. "Seriously, piggy, you twitch funny and I'm taking off your stupid foot." She thumped his leg a few times to make her point. "Blow it right the hell off. Test me." She bared her teeth and stared hard into his eyes. He had to know she meant it. "Please."

When he was finally calmed down a bit, Theresa let Warburton lead the way. His knees shook, but he walked.

Chapter Forty

Cody Laurel/Hank

WHAT'S HAPPENING?

You heard. We're dying.

I don't want to die.

How do you think I feel, Cody? I've barely had two weeks here.

You've been around a little longer than that.

Yes, I have, but I haven't been active. Mostly I've been stuck sleeping inside of you. There was no resentment, just explanation.

So how do we fix this?

One of us is going to have to die, I think. If we keep changing, we're going to fall apart.

What do you mean? He didn't want to die. He wanted to get home to his parents and pretend this had never happened. There were video games to play, and a fervent hope that someday he would actually kiss a girl—hell—maybe even get to second base.

Can't you feel it? Bad things are happening inside of us. Of course he felt it. The pain was there constantly. And the cold.

How do we decide?

Why don't we just let the body decide?

How, Hank?

Just . . . just let it happen. Whatever the body decides, we just have to go with it.

I'm scared. If he couldn't be truthful with himself, who could he be truthful with? And, okay, so Hank was maybe not completely him, but he was definitely part of the equation.

Me too. I don't want to die. Cody took comfort in that knowledge. If dying scared Hank too, maybe Cody wasn't the world's biggest wimp. Just, you know, a contender.

So don't.

Might not have a choice.

Maybe we do.

What do you mean? He could feel Hank's curiosity, sense that he had his Other's attention.

Let the body decide. But don't give up on the mind.

Close your eyes. It's time. Let's get this done.

They closed their eyes just as the alarms sounded.

Chapter Forty-One

Not-Kyrie

NOT-KYRIE CARRIED CODY with ease; but his body was changing again and that meant she was losing the fight to haul around his deadweight. They were out in the hallway and running as much as they could. But the place was laid out like a maze, and they had no idea where the hell they were, as Sam kept pointing out again and again.

"You have to carry him. He's getting too heavy." She bent at the waist to set Cody down. Even as she did, his legs worked and he was standing. His body was weak and shaking, but he was standing. It was something.

"I'm good." His voice sounded all wrong. Not Cody, not Hank, but something different.

His body had stabilized a bit too, locked halfway between the transformations. The skin around his eyes looked dark and bruised, and his flesh was pasty to the point of resembling clown makeup, but he was conscious.

"Are you okay?"

Hank shook his head. In her heart she knew it was Hank looking at her, not Cody. He was too calm to be Cody. "Feel like shit, but I'm up. Let's go. We have to get to the west side of the building."

"Why?" That was Sam.

"Theresa is here. She's trying to break us out." He walked as he spoke, and without even being aware of it, the other two followed him.

"Wait. Who is Theresa?" Not-Kyrie asked.

"Not-Tina. She gave herself a name." Not-Kyrie frowned, and when she did, Hank 2.0 gave a grin that was pure Cody. "Looks like you're behind the curve on this one."

She hadn't known either of the boys for very long, but what she was talking to was enough of Hank and of Cody that it was unsettling. Then he looked away from her and turned abruptly down a corridor that veered to the left.

Sam was right behind her and glancing in every direction at once. "We need to get the hell out of here. Seriously. There are guards."

"I know. I can hear some of them coming. Get ready."

Sam nodded and listened, scowling. He was angry, she knew that, but he was also excited. They all were. They were bred for this: for danger and violence. It was a part of what made them what they were, whatever *that* really was.

That was what they'd hoped to discover, after all.

Sam handed her a dart gun. "Whatever's in these things, it'll give us at least one less target when it hits, right?"

She took the weapon and flipped it in her hand a couple of times as she moved, examining the trigger and the barrel. Definitely not a regular gun, but if it fired, it would probably cause someone a world of hurt. It was good enough for her.

Hank was almost out of range and she moved to catch up with him, frowning again, puzzled. He moved like he knew where he was going, but that was impossible.

Wasn't it?

Chapter Forty-Two

Joe Bronx

HE PUSHED BACK A strange sense of déjà vu as the guard opened the door to his cell. The alarms echoed madly in the hallway, and he could see lights flashing in the distance, even from his vantage point.

The guard looked at the empty bed and then looked around the room. Joe was bigger than he had been the last time he'd hidden in the corner of the ceiling, so the guard spotted him around the same time Joe landed on his face. Had he been using his brain, he would have looked into the room through the two-way glass, but he wasn't that damned smart.

The next guard wasn't much brighter. He was reaching for a large red button on the side of the hallway wall as Joe lunged at him. As if hitting the alarm would make a difference now that the alarms were already screaming.

He hit the button at the same time Joe hit his face. The man's face shattered. The wall button had just sent an electrical impulse that started the alarms. Too late.

There were five men total who came to Joe's door. The greeter and the button pusher were down and broken before the others knew what was happening. The other three had a bad problem on their hands.

Joe was feeling a little like shedding blood.

One of them had a gun. Not a normal gun, but something that was designed for short ranges. Joe could smell chemicals coming from the barrel. Just to make sure he didn't get any new chemicals added to the stew, he grabbed the hand holding the gun and wrenched it to the side. A dart fired from the tip and bounced off the wall. The jerk with the gun watched the dart as it flew, like his entire life depended on it somehow pulling a fast one and flying at Joe all by itself.

While he was watching the dart, Joe kicked him in the chest. The man barely had time to grunt before he was bouncing off the wall too. That left two guards, both of whom were smarter than their companions. They tried to run.

Joe let them live, but he made sure they didn't try to get any more help. They bounced off the walls hard enough to break a few bones, but not hard enough to suffer brain trauma.

He listened with his ears and with his mind. The alarms

drowned out almost everything else, and he still couldn't hear the others in his head. The silence enraged him. Was it the drugs? Had Evelyn and her vile minions killed all of his new family? He didn't know, but the thought festered inside of him like a slow-moving poison and made him angrier still.

Evelyn Hope. She'd be coming soon. He knew that. No way would she be far off. She needed to see him, to watch him die. He knew that in his heart. Especially if she had killed his people. She'd want him to know first. How did he know that? Because it was what he'd want. He'd want to see her suffer before she died. How different was he from the only woman he could ever call his mother?

Enough. It was time to leave.

Joe looked the people over and saw no weapons, save more dart guns. They'd come to subdue him and little more. Not surprising, really.

He grabbed two of the guns. One he tucked under his arm. The other one, he had different plans for. He opened the cylinder and pulled out the first two of the four darts inside. A few seconds later he threw the emptied syringes to the ground.

Time to go. Time to finish this.

"Evelyn? Are you listening?" He looked around the hallway until he spotted what he'd known would be there. A video camera. "Can you hear me, Mother? I'm coming for you. This is over!"

He ran past the camera and darted to the right at the first intersection. He had no idea where he was going, but he had to go somewhere. He'd find someone to give him directions soon enough.

Chapter Forty-Three

Evelyn Hope

"GABRIEL?"

Gabby looked up at her and blinked the sleep from his eyes. "Yeah, Mom?"

"Does the moon always shine so brightly at noon?" Evelyn closed her eyes. She didn't want to see him change. She wanted to see her baby boy, not the soldier he became. Still, that was a luxury she was not allowed just then.

Rafael stood at attention, his body rigid, his posture perfect.

"Yes, ma'am?" He didn't question the clothes he was in. He didn't ask for explanations. Rafael was a good soldier. In return, she was all business.

"I need you to assemble your team. Subject Seven has escaped. Get him. Get him now and take him down."

"Do you want him alive?"

A damned fine question, that. "Preferably. Use the command phrase. Drop him as quickly as you can. But if it's him or you, kill him."

Rafael nodded as he slipped into his shoes. "Yes, ma'am."

He left the suite they were staying in. He already knew the way to the barracks for the others. Their control parents had not come on the trip, so they stayed together in a separate area. By rights, Rafael should have been with them, but Evelyn wanted the comfort of having her son closer. And now she was sending him off again to fight against her other son. A monster. Her stomach roiled at the notion, her heart pounded in her chest. She hated this.

But at least he wouldn't be alone. He'd be with five other armed and highly trained soldiers who were capable of bench pressing in excess of seven hundred pounds each. That thought should have comforted her, and yet she still felt the butterflies trying to tear her stomach apart.

Seven wouldn't live through the night if everything went the way it should. Bobby would be dead, but that was a tragic necessity. If a sacrifice had to be made, she preferred losing Bobby to Gabriel.

Just in case, she double-checked her weapons. If he did get past Rafael's Strike Team, he would be coming for her. She knew that. In her very soul, she knew that. And this time, she would be ready for him.

George entered the room without asking, his face pale

and his mouth drawn down in a tight line. He was scared. He had every reason to be.

Just the same, the hand that held his pistol didn't shake in the least as he checked it again.

"Let's get to the office, George. The doors there are armored."

George nodded and started down the hallway. That was good. She wasn't sure if she could remember the way to the office.

Fear did that to a person. Made one forget things.

And she was so damned afraid.

Chapter Forty-Four

Theresa

WARBURTON STOPPED WHEN HIS phone started ringing, and Theresa stopped too, looking at him as if he'd lost his freaking mind.

"Okay, seriously?"

"What? I have to answer it." He was sounding awfully defensive.

"Rules ain't changed. You say a word about me, I'll blow that foot right off your leg."

He nodded, but he looked annoyed. He was starting to think she was a joke, and that pissed her off.

"Evelyn, yes. I'm here. I just got here. What's going on? Why the alarms?" He nodded in response. "Yes, well, there was no one at the main desk. I waltzed in here like I owned the place. Yes, I'm aware that I own the place, which is why I'm firing whoever was supposed to be in reception."

Seriously? She stared at him. These guys were idiots.

Warburton started pacing. "Evelyn, none of the Doppelgangers here are ready for combat. You know that. It's going to be your kids or no one."

How many of us did they make? She wasn't sure she wanted to know.

He looked back at her—a nervous flicker of his eyes—and licked his lips. And she knew right then that she should have been paying better attention to what was going on around her, because damned if she didn't know at that exact second that he'd betrayed her with some comment or code phrase.

He had the same problem that everyone had: he thought she was stupid. Tina wasn't dumb, and neither was Theresa. Tina knew enough to watch the made men around her and to understand more about them than they realized. Her common sense gave Theresa an edge. Theresa knew what Tina knew.

She turned her head just in time to see the attackers coming for her from behind, all of them moving fast and trying to be quiet, a task made easier by the alarms going off.

She saw them. They saw her. She fired first. The weapon had a lot more kick than she'd expected, and the first bullet blew a hole in the wall next to the first man in line. He let out a yelp and she fired a second time, compensating for the explosive power of the weapon. The bullet struck the man in his hip and spun him around before he hit the ground. Long before that time came to pass, Theresa had aimed and fired twice more. Two more guards fell to the ground. She didn't bother to see if they were dead or alive. All that mattered to her was that they were no longer an immediate threat.

By the time she turned back to Warburton, he was running, his little body jiggling and wiggling and panting as he ran for all he was worth. When Tina was a kid, she'd watched footage of a panther taking down a deer in the middle of some sort of jungle. Theresa remembered it only in flashes, but she could access the images if she tried. She felt like that cat as she charged, covering the distance between the two of them in a second.

She leaped and landed on Warburton, her unexpected weight on his upper back staggering him and sending him to his knees. He fell hard and grunted and cried out as he dropped to the ground. She moved away from him, landing on her feet and stopping her forward momentum with ease.

Warburton was panting hard when she walked up to his prone body. He looked back at her with wide, tearing eyes.

Tina would have pissed herself. She wasn't strong. Not like Theresa was. Theresa knew that, even if Tina didn't. Lucky for both of them, it was Theresa in charge right then.

"What the hell did I tell you I was gonna do?" She hissed the words past clenched teeth.

"I. Please. I didn't."

The bullet slammed into Warburton's ankle at high speed, and lead expanded as it hit the bone. The bone shattered. Warburton screamed as the impact shredded his foot into a ruin of meat and bone.

"You're useless! I should kill you!" Her rage grew. The more he screamed, the more she hated him for his weakness. This little pig was one of the people responsible for creating her? The idea made her sick. "I should kill your wife and your kids! Give me a reason not to kill them, you stupid loser!"

He was beyond the ability to speak. Josh Warburton was screaming in pain and holding what was left of his leg in an effort to stop the bleeding.

Without another word, Theresa turned away from him. He was nothing. Less than nothing.

She had things to do.

Theresa. We need you.

"Tell me where I'm going."

The voice didn't respond with words. Instead she felt a tug in her mind, telling her what direction to go. She followed the feeling, moving toward the left as soon as she could. As she moved, she did her best to keep her eyes and ears open, and she also pulled two more prizes from her bag of weapons. Only one of them had bullets. The other was much worse.

When she heard the sound of moving feet, she stopped and slid against the wall. The noises were coming from ahead of her, at the closest intersection, and from the right. The odd pulling sensation in her head was still coming from her left, meaning that the noises probably weren't coming from her friends.

She was half right.

A man in a black uniform sailed through the air at the intersection screaming the entire way, at least until the wall stopped him. He crumpled to the ground in a broken pile, and a second later Joe came into her view, his face set in a savage sneer and his hands already covered with blood.

Despite the situation, she felt her blood pressure surge. Damn, he was a handsome sight, even in the worst of situations. Maybe because of the situation. She didn't know. She just knew he confused her.

He looked directly at her and shook his head. It wasn't a sign that he didn't want to see her, but a quick communication. His eyes told her there were plenty of opponents coming and that if she stepped into the mess he'd made, she'd be in for a world of trouble.

Theresa nodded and tossed one of her guns toward him. Joe grinned as he snatched the weapon out of the air and dropped to the ground at the same time. He rolled his body to the side and crouched against the wall, looking back the way he'd come.

A moment later he was moving, charging toward whatever was chasing him. She heard the sound of the gun firing again and again, but the noise was quickly swallowed by Joe's roar of anger.

Theresa wanted to go to him, but the insistent tug in her mind pulled harder, making her look in the other direction. Despite her desires, she turned from Joe at the intersection, drawn to the call of the other voice.

She glanced back and saw no sign of Joe—just the bodies he'd left behind.

Chapter Forty-Five

Joe Bronx

THEY WERE EVERYWHERE, LIKE cockroaches. He knew about roaches. The damned things had come out of the woodwork in half the hotels he'd called home in the last five years.

The guards came for him, some of them moving cautiously, some of them braver than they were smart, all of them armed and trying to take him down.

And he reveled in it. They charged at him and Joe struck them down, knocking them aside or bending them until they broke, whichever served his purpose at that moment.

He should have been exhausted, but his body was singing with adrenaline and he felt as alive as he ever had. Not-Tina was an unexpected surprise. He fired four bullets at the crowd of guards coming for him and let out a battle cry at the same time. They did the sensible thing and broke ranks.

The hallways were not overly wide, and they knew that the bullets he fired would find targets if they kept coming for him. Two of the rounds hit people and dropped them, dead or wounded. He charged past and held the weapon where they could all see it. They wisely ran away from him.

And then the hallway was empty for a moment. Joe listened, studying its length, trying to figure out what would happen next. He still didn't know where the hell he was or how to get out. Of course, he had things to take care of before he left, but still, it would have been good to know how to escape when the time came.

The ceiling was solid. Instead of acoustic tiles, there was merely concrete. No way to easily escape from being seen, no way to sneak past the cameras. And there were cameras everywhere.

Damn.

A face peered around the corner, and he almost took a shot but stopped himself when he recognized the features. It was one of the Doppelgangers, one of the ones designed to replace him. She was looking at him with a cold, careful stare, taking his measure. He took careful aim and fired at the spot between her eyes. She was fast enough to get away, which was exactly what he'd expected.

Five bullets gone, which meant twelve more if he was lucky.

The girl came back into view along with two more, all

three of them armed, and none of them carrying the dart guns. They were using real guns with real bullets. Damn.

There wasn't much choice in the matter. He either retreated from them and risked getting shot in the back, or he charged toward them and cut loose with everything he had. Neither idea had much appeal, but the notion of dying a coward's death was far worse.

"I'm coming for you!" He made sure his voice was loud and clear, and he punctuated the sentence with a bullet. The same girl he'd missed before didn't quite get clear a second time and he saw a wound open in her shoulder where the bullet passed through meat.

The girl screamed and the oversized male with her took careful aim and fired. Joe had the same luck as the girl. He felt a bullet crease his side just under his arm as he charged. He didn't let himself flinch, but instead took aim and fired again, aiming for the bastard with the decent marksmanship. His bullet blew a hole in the loser's stomach. The weapon fell from the bruiser's hands and he scrambled to cover the wound in his guts.

Joe had killed many times in his life, but never one of his own kind. He felt an odd twinge of guilt as he took aim again and fired a second round at the boy holding his insides in place.

The second bullet was a killing shot.

The third Doppelganger cut loose with a hail of bullets.

Her weapon was automatic, and she didn't waste time taking careful aim. Instead she fired a spray of bullets toward him as she screamed her rage in his direction.

Adrenaline roared through Joe's body and he ignored the pain as three bullets slapped into him. None of them were lethal, but all of them were painful. He should have run away, he knew that, but instead Joe charged, loping forward like an ape until he reached the girl with the trigger finger and slammed into her with his full strength. She was a Doppelganger—that meant increased strength and reflexes—but like him she was furious and that made her foolish. He was wounded, bleeding and exhausted.

Joe smashed her into the wall hard enough to break bones. She did not scream, but instead let out a small gasp before she collapsed. He didn't stop to think about her. Instead he looked to the other girl—the one he'd winged—and fired at her again from less than four feet away.

Like her boyfriend before her, she fell down, very likely dead or dying.

Joe stared down at the bodies for a moment and panted, his blood singing, his wounds wailing their agony into his system.

Three down. Two dead, one broken. He shook his head. Not what he wanted. He wanted them working with him, not dying because of him.

Still, he was standing and his enemies were falling. That

was what mattered.

A camera looked blindly at him from twenty feet away. He hoped Evelyn was looking on, watching him destroy all she had worked so hard for.

"I'm coming for you, Evelyn!"

He didn't wait around to see if she would respond—for all he knew there were intercoms in the damned place. Joe grabbed the weapons he could and ran, headed for Evelyn Hope and the answers to his questions. His blood fell from open wounds, and still he charged forward.

This was going to end, one way or another.

Chapter Forty-Six

Evelyn Hope

EVELYN WATCHED THREE OF her best—Sean, Mary, and Tori—fall to Seven and felt a shiver run down her back.

"That. He can't just." George was having trouble making a full sentence.

"He can. He did." And really, right then, at that moment, she knew he had to die. It hurt her, but she couldn't let him stay around any longer. Subject Seven was simply too dangerous to let live, even if it meant she had to say goodbye to Bobby again, once and for all. She forced the threatening tears back and got to work.

She looked at the security monitors. On one of the screens, two members of security were dragging Josh off the floor and heading for medical as quickly as they could. He was screaming and thrashing. She could understand that. He was in agony. She could see how badly ruined his foot was, even on a small black-and-white screen.

On another screen, she saw Rafael react to his people falling to Seven. He didn't crumble as she'd feared, but she could see him screaming at his subordinates. He was angry, and that was good. That was important, because the Doppelgangers worked best when they were angry. They were designed to think better and faster when they were enraged than when they were afraid. That was one of the things that made them such good soldiers. Fear wasn't exactly alien to them, but it wasn't the way they were wired to think and feel. They had been designed to be perfect stealth weapons and perfect killing machines, and that meant they functioned better in situations that would have left most human soldiers crippled.

And she needed Rafael angry. She needed him capable of thinking and reacting faster than Seven.

She slipped the headset on quickly and tapped the access code into her keyboard.

"Rafael."

"Yes." His voice was curt and hard. Good.

"He's injured. Yes, he's hurt—maybe even killed—some of your people, but they hurt him. Act quickly and you can take him down, do you hear me?"

He looked around. "Where is he?"

"North wing. Heading for the center of the compound."

"He's mine. Get everyone out of my way." It wasn't

a request. He wanted Seven dead.

"Don't forget the command phrase. Take him down hard and fast, before he can kill anyone else."

Rafael didn't answer. Instead he charged toward the north wing as quickly as he could, his two remaining Strikers in tow, both looking as ready for a fight as he was.

Chapter Forty-Seven

Hank

HANK STAGGERED, HIS LEGS weak, his head swimming. His eyes refused to focus properly, and the only reason he was able to see worth a damn was because he was seeing from Not-Kyrie and Sam's perspectives. It was disorienting, but he was able to view the world from their eyes and from Theresa's as well.

None of which made it any easier for him to keep his balance. If that was what Joe went through, he had to admire the bastard's self-control.

But there was no time for that. He had to get them out of this place and quickly, because he could feel his body and his mind trying to fall apart. Cody was whispering in his head constantly and that was a comfort, but it challenged his ability to focus. Maybe he was going to die—he was almost certain that he was—but he wanted them safe first.

That was important. He needed them safe, because then dying would at least have a decent purpose.

Not that he didn't prefer living, of course.

He could sense Theresa coming closer. That was good. That was a big plus.

"She's coming. She's almost here."

"How the hell do you *know* that?" Sam was staring hard at him.

"I can smell her, too." Not-Kyrie. He understood something that even she didn't really get. Her senses were insane. He knew he could hear, see, and smell far better than Cody, but in comparison to Not-Kyrie, he was almost blind and deaf. He didn't clarify but instead savored the puzzled look on Sam's face. Sam was trouble. He had to think about whether or not he was going to tell the others about the boy betraying them. In any event, it would have to wait.

Theresa was almost there, and he could hear her being chased.

Bring them around the corner. Come left and then duck, okay? He spoke without words. She answered with words and thoughts, not aware that he didn't actually need the words.

She's coming. Take aim. Be ready.

They both nodded and all three of them took careful aim with the dart guns they'd liberated.

Theresa came in low and fast, literally running on all

fours. She bounded around the corner at high speed and stayed low. They waited and fired as one, spurred on by Hank's mental commands.

The darts shot through the air and nailed the guards. Hank's target took one in the shoulder, Sam's in the chest and Not-Kyrie's got a dart in the side of his face and let out a scream worthy of a cranky baby.

All three of them were falling by the time the next group came around the corner.

How many?

"Lots!" Theresa answered, getting back to her feet. She dug around in a sack slung over her shoulder and danced out of the way of the three of them as she kept searching. "I got a grenade in here somewhere. Hang on."

"A grenade?! Have you lost your mind?" Sam's voice cracked, but Hank could also sense a thrill in the other boy's mind. He wanted to know how much damage a grenade would do to their enemies.

"We're in a hallway. Blow up the walls, and this place comes down on us." Hank moved closer to the corner and took a look around the edge, assessing the damage as best he could, despite the way the room wanted to swim. He didn't get a clear count, but there were twenty or more men in uniforms down that way.

Theresa moved up next to him and threw her grenade. It bounced and spun and rolled down the hallway and Hank felt his eyes grow to the size of saucers in his head. She'd actually thrown the damned thing, even after he warned against it.

"It's a concussion grenade. Big noise, no explosion. Run." Her voice was very direct and carried an edge of excitement.

Hank turned fast enough to make the hallway swim faster and started running. He could hear the guards down the hallway from them screaming as they realized what had been thrown.

Hank ran, and Not-Kyrie was right there, grabbing his arm and guiding him on, urging him to move faster and faster.

And then the noise came and the air vanished from around them for a few seconds as the grenade detonated. He felt like he was floating for just a second, and then he felt nothing at all.

Chapter Forty-Eight

Sam Hall

SAM LOOKED DOWN AT Hank as the smoke cleared. The impact had been bad, but not rough enough to drop the other boy. He wasn't well, and that was all there was to it. As Sam looked Hank over, Theresa and Not-Kyrie both stood back up.

A quick calculation: Theresa was facing the other direction and holding her head. The noise and concussive force had stunned her. Not-Kyrie was worse. If he was right, she was more sensitive to sound than any of the rest of them, and for her that meant it must have been like getting swatted by the world's biggest baseball bat.

Hank still wasn't moving. His head was turned just enough that if he'd been conscious, he would have moved it. It was at the sort of angle where one quick stomp on the back of his head would either kill him outright or leave him paralyzed. Especially a kick coming from someone strong enough to knock down an oak door, like Sam.

The only person who could point out that he'd betrayed them was down and out. If he was smart about it, he'd finish him off.

It was simple math, really.

"Damn it." He mumbled the words as he grabbed Hank and slung the larger boy over his shoulder. "Let's go! Places to be and all that crap!" He barely looked at the girls as he started moving. They needed to be elsewhere; that was all there was to it.

Chapter Forty-Nine

Evelyn Hope

EVELYN TALKED TO THE medics as she watched the animals running free in her zoo. Josh's foot was a loss. They'd be amputating. It was that or let him bleed out.

Despite her fears, Seven had only wounded the Strike Team members. It was easy to forget exactly how tough they were. They were out of commission, but if the surgeries went well, they'd probably recover completely, given enough time to rest.

This was starting to look up a bit, and that scared the hell out of her. Where Seven was concerned, it was best to assume the worst at all times. He was . . . well, he was a monster. She knew it and couldn't stop thinking it.

George cleared his throat and pointed to the monitors. Rafael was closing in on Seven. The thought made her pulse race.

"He's ahead of you on the right, Rafael. Next corridor, halfway down the hall." She spoke into the headset that communicated directly with Gabby's Doppelganger and felt her muscles tense at the thought. Gabby loved Bobby. Gabby adored and revered the memories of his older brother, who was both hero and figure of legend in his mind. For years she had filled his head with tales of his older brother when it was bedtime. Gabriel was such a sweet boy. She knew in her head that Rafael was not as kind or as gentle. Her heart? That was a different story. He was a fighter, and a damned skilled one. She'd watched him take on ten men in heavily padded armor and mop the floor with them on a few occasions. He was well trained and designed to be as fierce as Seven. Truth be told, he was closer to Seven than a lot of the others, because like Seven he was an Alpha, and they were naturally stronger and faster than their counterparts, a happy coincidence that helped them keep control in almost any situation.

He had guns, body armor and the command phrase that would turn Seven into Bobby, stripping him of all of his combat knowledge and a good deal of his aggressiveness. He had every advantage, besides having two more of the Strike Team with him.

And she was still ready to pee her pants thinking about him going up against Seven.

"Be careful."

Rafael didn't answer, but he nodded, letting her know he'd heard her. Seven was too close by, and speaking would alert the enemy.

George spoke up, pointing his hand at another monitor. She was reminded again that he was the best assistant she could have ever asked for. Without being told to, he was keeping her up on the location of all the players in their drama. The rest of Seven's collection of rejects was moving toward the exit. That would not do. A quick tap of a few buttons sent the elevator up to the surface level, removing their chance for an easy method of escape. The car would not move from that location until she typed in another code, and she had no intention of doing so. She wasn't that foolish.

They weren't going anywhere. She and the rest of her people had learned from previous mistakes with Seven. No escapes, not ever.

"Tell me again why we never put a damned intercom system in this station, George?" With a proper intercom she could have ended this. A simple command phrase and Seven would have been down and out. The information was classified, of course, but she doubted many people would have remembered the words. The phrases were set up to be awkward, nonsensical configurations that wouldn't be easy to recall.

"Why else? Security. PA systems hardly lead to good

security." He sniffed as he spoke, and she knew that he was resisting the temptation to say he'd told her so, which he had. That was for the best. She was currently armed and in exactly a bad enough a mood to wing him if he decided to be an ass.

Instead of pulling the trigger, she quickly keyed into her communications and called for security to head for the elevator. "Bring out the real artillery. They are now armed. Shoot to kill." She didn't wait for a response but immediately switched channels again. "Right around the corner, Rafael. You'll have visual in a moment."

Rafael nodded, impatiently this time, and though she had no idea what he said, his Strike Team immediately crouched a bit lower, their hands holding their weapons.

It was time.

Evelyn licked her lips, which were suddenly too damned dry.

It was time for Seven to die.

Chapter Fifty

Joe Bronx

JOE SAVORED THE SOUND of the alarms for a moment, knowing that in a few seconds they would be gone. He reached into his pocket for the darts he'd set aside earlier.

This was going to hurt like hell.

They were trying to be quiet, but they were failing. The sounds that three people walking made might be missed by most people—especially in a crisis where there were sirens and alarm bells making enough noise to drive a person half mad—but Joe wasn't like most people. He'd spent years listening, studying the sounds around him in almost every environment. He heard them as they carefully came toward him, and more importantly, he smelled them. He knew their scents from earlier. Gabby was among them. Not Gabby, but his Other. The strong one, who knew the right words to force him to sleep.

If he weren't an Alpha, it was possible that Gabby's Other would have been able to put him to sleep with only a thought. He could have projected the catchphrase into Joe's mind and made him fall into the nothing that existed when Hunter was free. At least that was what he'd been told once by the man who'd told him all about the rest of the Failures before he'd been forced to kill him.

Even if Gabby had been able to force the command phrase into his mind under most circumstances, the idiots had taken care of that for him when they drugged him. He couldn't hear his own people and they couldn't hear him. That also meant that Gabby's Hyde couldn't hear his mental thoughts.

And that meant there was only one way to get the words into Joe's mind. The old-fashioned way: by speaking.

With that in mind, Joe braced himself for the pain and shoved the darts into his ears, forcing himself to go against his own instincts for self-preservation until he felt the needle tips burst his eardrums. There was an explosion of pain (and he thought he might have screamed), then there was complete silence.

And then they were coming around the corner, charging him, furious at him for what he had already done to their friends.

Like he cared.

Joe grinned and charged them with the same fury. They'd

taken from him too. They'd stolen his new friends from him, taken his voice and his power, and they'd beaten him down. He could have forgiven almost anything, but the last was a sin he could not let go unpunished.

It's said that in times of extreme stress, the world seems to slow down: adrenaline drives the senses into overdrive and the sensory input is so intense that the mind can barely take it all in. There had been very few occasions in Subject Seven's life where that was true; this moment was one of them. Despite being deafened, he was aware of everything around him.

They came toward him with bared teeth, flared nostrils and wide, dilated eyes that saw everything as well as he did. The weapons in their hands were designed to kill, not to stun.

Gabby's Other was screaming, but the words were lost on Joe. Gabby's mouth moved and he bellowed the words with harsh breaths, but to no avail.

The boy faltered for a moment, uncertain why his command phrase was failing.

Joe took aim as his "brother" hesitated. He fired at the subordinate male on the left of the leader. The one who was firing back at him.

Both of them were too close to make ducking even a remote possibility. Seven let out a yelp as the bullet caught him across his cheek, slashing his face. The boy was cocky. He went for a head shot.

Joe fired at the chest. He hit clean and watched the boy fly backward as the force of the bullet threw him into reverse. He only had a few choices. He could jump to one side, drop low, go high or charge straight ahead. He dropped low and let himself hit the ground as the bullets cut a path where he had been only a second before. From his angle on the ground, he fired at the pretty blonde girl looking at him. She bore a resemblance to Not-Kyrie, but that was hardly surprising. They were all from the same basic genetic stock, weren't they?

Two bullets hit the girl. One in the ribs and one in the throat. She smashed into the closest wall and left a thick tide of blood dripping down the paint. Joe didn't dare let himself think about her. There was still Gabby's Other to consider.

The boy kicked him in the face hard enough to bust his nose and very possibly break a bone or two. It was hard to say for certain.

The gun dropped from Joe's hand. He looked up just in time to see Gabby's Hyde kicking at his face again. No time to block, so he lowered his head and felt the steel-toed boot bounce off the top of his skull. The pain was immediate and intense. He couldn't let that stop him. The only reason he was alive was because Gabby was too angry to think. If he took two steps back, he could have shot Joe and there would have been nothing Joe could have done to stop him.

Instead he tried kicking a third time, and Joe launched himself from his prone position, driving into the other boy with all of his strength and screaming and snapping and clawing with his fingers.

Gabriel Hope was a well-trained combatant. His Doppelganger shared all of the combat knowledge and had the strength and reflexes to make him formidable indeed. He defended himself well, blocking with efficient blows that would have staggered a heavyweight boxer.

Subject Seven—Joe—had spent five years on the streets, on his own, making a living any way he could, and that often meant fighting men twice his size in street brawls for cash. He had also had to defend himself from literally hundreds of people over the years who wanted to take what was his from him and didn't understand that his willingness to fight back was second only to his raw strength and savagery.

Rafael defended himself again and again, while Joe attacked relentlessly, pushing the other boy backward with repeated blows and sheer brute force.

Rafael smashed an elbow into Joe's chin and throat and would have crushed his windpipe if Joe hadn't turned his head in time. In response, Joe raked his fingers across Rafael's face, his nails scratching both of the other boy's eyes and leaving red welts across his face.

Rafael screamed, momentarily blinded, and Joe cut loose

on him. He grabbed the other boy's hair and shoved his head into the wall with a resounding thump. As the Other tried to recover, Joe did it again and again until finally Rafael sagged, stunned beyond his ability to regenerate.

There was no time to think. If he thought, there was a chance that Hunter would resurface and fight him and he could not allow that. Instead Joe ran back down the hallway and grabbed the gun he'd been carrying before.

"You could have stopped this, Evelyn!" He could barely hear himself, but by the scratch in his throat he knew he was yelling. "You could have worked something out with me! You did this! This is all your fault!" He meant the words, too. He'd wanted his freedom. He'd been naive to think she would forgive him, but he'd been willing to let the past go in exchange for simply getting rid of Hunter. He'd have been satisfied with that, despite his hatred for the woman who'd been his captor for most of his life. He'd have let go of his grudge against her if she'd been willing to help him. Now it had come to this. There were so many things he wanted, but he could have accepted a compromise.

His heart pounded and adrenaline sang through his body and made him shake. His body ached from repeated gunshot wounds and from the battering he'd received at Gabby's hands.

"What happens to little Gabby when I blow this bastard's head off, Mommy? You gonna bring him back? You miss

Bobby? Say goodbye to the other one!"

His mouth was bared and spittle fell from his lips. He reached down and grabbed Gabby's Other, smelling the scent of Evelyn Hope's perfume past the smell of blood and violence and sweat. The boy was covered with her scent, and that notion fueled his anger as little else could have.

He shoved the gun against Gabby's temple.

"Hey, Mommy! This one's just for you!"

Joe pulled the trigger.

Chapter Fifty-One

Evelyn Hope

SHE WANTED TO BELIEVE it was a joke or a modified piece of footage. She wanted desperately to believe that she was dreaming, but the feeling of her hands dragging down her face and clutching at the chain that held a single tooth and a wedding ring convinced her that she was awake and that what she had seen was reality.

There was no two ways about it. There was no chance of error. Rafael fell to the floor with a gaping wound in his skull. She was a doctor. She knew the signs. He wasn't unconscious. He was dead.

Rafael was dead.

Gabriel was dead.

Gabby was dead.

Her little boy was dead.

She looked at the monitor and stared past the ruined body

to look instead at the wild-eyed boy who stared back at the camera mounted to the wall at ceiling height. He screamed and he smiled, and he held out the gun that had killed her baby boy, and he let it drop to the ground.

And then Subject Seven turned away from the camera and ran down the corridor.

Leaving Evelyn to stare at the remains of her family, dead and cooling on the floor of the world she had helped create.

She wanted so much to scream, but she could not find the breath to make a noise.

And George, God above love him, was there, urging her away from the cameras that showed her the destruction of everything that mattered to her.

She couldn't feel her face, couldn't catch a breath.

Couldn't think or feel anything at all, because the truth was too big for her to escape.

Gabby was dead.

Bobby had killed him.

Chapter Fifty-Two

Sam Hall

ONE SECOND HANK WAS deadweight, and the next he shook violently and struggled until Sam set him on his feet.

"We're leaving. I have him. I can feel him."

"Feel who?" Theresa frowned and rechecked the clip on her pistol. Like it had somehow unloaded itself in the last fifteen seconds since the last time she'd checked it.

"Joe. He's out there and coming here, but he's going somewhere else first."

"We should meet him." That was Theresa again.

Not-Kyrie nodded her agreement. "Let's go."

"No." Hank shook his head. "We need to get this elevator shaft open."

"Car's stuck." Theresa shrugged as if that was the end of the matter.

"Then we have to get past it. I don't care if we punch

through the bottom of the damned thing, we have to get out of here."

Sam stared hard at him, a cold feeling growing in his stomach. "Why?"

"Because Joe did a bad thing, and they're going to kill us if they can." Hank had a strange, faraway look on his face as he spoke. Like he wasn't really with them but was looking elsewhere and just happened to hear them and respond.

"What the hell are you talking about?" Sam felt his temper rising. He didn't like the way Hank was acting, not one bit. It made him nervous, and that in turn made him irritable.

Not-Kyrie lifted her hands. "Whatever. Help me with the damn doors."

Hank reached out and grabbed at the sliding doors. They fought and groaned as he pushed, but he pushed back all the harder and slowly forced the doors to separate. When he'd finally made enough room for her, Not-Kyrie slipped through the opening and Theresa followed suit, bracing the open doors with her body. The doors wanted to close, but the body blocking them prevented it. Maybe someone had been cut in half by closing elevators doors in the past. Sam wasn't really sure. After almost a minute the elevator started ringing with an alarm of its own, which was easily drowned out by all of the other noises.

"Sam, block the door, please. I think they're sending

guards for us." Hank sounded a little more like himself—which is to say more like he was in the room with the rest of them, because his new voice still didn't quite sound right. There was still a little bit of Cody in that voice.

Sam checked his pistol—eat your heart out, Theresa—and headed for the door to the small room. He looked to his left and almost got his head blown off by a bullet for his trouble. Four men in body armor were standing a distance away, and one of them had taken a shot at him.

"Hey, Theresa?"

"Yeah?" Her voice was muffled by the elevator alarm, but he heard her clearly enough.

"Got any more of those grenades?"

"What, are you high? Those things cost money. I was lucky to get one." He looked over his shoulder and saw her looking back at him.

"Yeah, well, armed guards with big guns over here. I could use a little help."

She let out a rude noise and pointed to Hank. "Come here and hold the damn door."

Hank looked at her for a second and finally nodded, moving over to replace her. He moved slowly, painfully—but he moved.

She watched his eyes looking her over and grinned. "You better watch what you think about me or I'll castrate you."

"What?" Hank sounded too defensive.

"Just get the hell over here," Sam said. He wasn't in the mood to watch the two of them flirt, if that was what they were doing. He couldn't quite tell, with Theresa.

Theresa rolled her eyes in his direction and stuck her tongue out but came over just the same.

"Which side?"

"Left."

"You go high. I go low." He nodded. "One. Two. Three."

They both leaned out of the door to the office at the same time and began firing. The people in the hallway did the same thing. They were wearing armor, but Sam and Theresa were mostly shielded by a wall. The sound of gunfire dwarfed every other noise for a moment.

One bullet hit a guard in the visor, and the back of his helmet exploded. He fell dead to the floor. Another of them took a bullet to the knee, and he screamed as he fell. The other two retreated, looking extremely nervous.

"Almost out of bullets here." Sam looked at Theresa expectantly.

"Yeah, well, don't come crying to me. I only got one spare clip left and I'm keeping it."

"I'm a better shot." It seemed like good logic to him.

"Hell you say. You see me take out the guy's head?"

"Okay, seriously? That was me, and you know it."

"It was not!" She had a shrill edge to her voice that made him want to scream, but he resisted the urge. "I got him fair and square."

"You said you were going low." Logic. He would win the day with logic.

"Not as low as you're going by trying to claim my kill." She clicked her tongue when she was disapproving, and he was rapidly learning to hate that noise. And unsettling as it was, he knew at that exact second that he'd made the right choice in saving Hank. Hank was like Theresa: part of his family, however warped that might be.

"Okay. You can keep the fresh clip. Give me the bullets left in your clip now so we can get the losers before they get to us."

"Not a chance."

She reached into her little bag again, which was now mostly empty. Inside was indeed another clip. There was also another pistol. She handed him the other weapon.

"Seriously? What the hell were we arguing here?"

"You being a loser."

He had no answer to that, so instead he leaned back out the door and fired at the remaining guards. Theresa joined in, calling out insults as she did.

Chapter Fifty-Three

Not-Kyrie

NOT-KYRIE KNEW NOTHING at all about elevators. She studied the bottom of the car for several seconds as she perched on the ladder running along the elevator shaft's wall. She decided she'd listen to Hank's earlier advice and braced her feet as best she could on the metal rung and then beat at the floor of the elevator. The bottom was made of metal. After a few failed attempts to cause any damage, she finally got inventive. It cost her two fingernails to unfasten the tightened bolts on the bottom of the car, but after that she was able to peel back the metal and punch her fist through the flooring.

And as she was beating the elevator into submission, she contemplated exactly what the hell they were doing. This was supposed to be a chance to get answers. Instead Hank had been poisoned somehow, Joe had disappeared, and

Not-Tina—*No,* she corrected herself, *Theresa*—had come up with a name. She'd been trusting Joe to give them a way to be free of their Others, and instead everything had gone wrong. Maybe it was time to seriously consider whether or not he was the right person to lead this group.

Kyrie wanted to go home. She knew that much about her Other without having to think. It was starting to sound like a damned fine idea. They could work out an arrangement of some kind. Anything would be better than going from one violent conflict to another. Yes, there was a part of her that wanted the violence— part of her that got off on beating the crap out of anyone who annoyed her—but not all of her. She wanted to choose who she fought and when, not answer to the whims of the people with her.

Since Joe had awakened her, she'd been involved in conflicts. She'd driven a tractor trailer across the country to deliver enough weapons for an army to Joe, and after that there had been shots fired, bodies beaten and broken, and little else.

Well, except for a few hellacious parties. That part she liked, because Kyrie was quite the little angel and didn't much think partying was a good idea.

She looked down at Hank far below her. "Got it."

Hank looked back up at her, and she studied his face for a moment. He was different now. The stressed expression was gone from his face, and the harsh features she'd come to associate with him had softened a bit. More importantly, he wasn't burning up from the inside anymore.

"We're just waiting on Joe. I can feel him. He's coming."

"You doing okay now, Hank?"

He looked up at her for a moment before he answered. "I think so. I think it's done."

"What's done?"

"Whatever was happening to me. I think I'm getting better." He looked away from her. "I don't know for sure."

"Better get up here. Just in case it isn't done with you."

"Someone's got to hold the door."

She shook her head. "Break the damn thing."

He stared at her as if the idea had never occurred to him. A moment later, he slammed his body against the door in its frame, and she heard the sound of metal crumpling into a new shape. Maybe Hank wasn't as big as he'd been before, but he was still insanely strong.

"Here I come." He looked at her and leered, but she knew he was only joking. This time at least. Hank was still a scary dude, even if she knew they were on the same side.

She grinned and climbed into the car. "Come get me if you can."

She didn't hear his response. She was too busy working on forcing the doors open from the inside.

Chapter Fifty-Four

Joe Bronx

OH, THE RAGE WAS burning so brightly! Joe's anger was a living thing. He'd wanted so much from this, a chance to see his mother, yes, but also a chance to get all of the information he needed on the rest of the Failures, the ones given up for adoption. He needed them, especially if he was going to win this little war he'd started.

Because it wasn't enough to make Evelyn cry. He wanted to ruin her. If she could not or would not help him, then he needed her to be beyond the point where she could make more like him. Joe needed to be unique. He could accept a few, a small number like him, so long as he was their leader. And being an Alpha almost guaranteed that. But the notion of an endless supply of others like him—only better trained—was not acceptable. Evelyn needed to be stopped. More importantly he needed to be the one who stopped her, because she needed to hate him as much as he hated her before he finally killed her, and she wasn't quite there yet. Not just yet, but hopefully soon.

He'd tried ten doors in the damnable place before he realized he could never find what he was looking for with guards everywhere and who knew how many Doppelgangers wandering around with weapons. Just because he had only seen six of them didn't mean there weren't more somewhere in the sprawling complex. How big was the place? If he had to hazard a guess, it was somewhere close to the size of a decent shopping mall. He couldn't be sure, because he had mostly run along corridors and through hallways and connecting passages.

He heard Hank's voice in his head, calling for him, and he finally decided to listen to it. Better to leave for now. He could find them again when the time came. It would take effort, but he was wounded—and badly, much worse than he wanted to admit. He was bleeding freely from too many wounds, and even with his constitution and strength he would falter soon. And then he would fall, if he wasn't extremely careful.

Almost as if to prove him right, his vision swam and started to gray for a second before he bit down on his tongue hard enough to make it bleed. The sudden pain helped him focus and move again, though he bounced off the wall before he finally made the last hallway between him and freedom. Two men were standing, facing a doorway where he could see Not-Tina and Sam, both of them with guns drawn and trying to get a good aim at the guards, who were now crouched down and trying to avoid being shot. Between the two groups, a couple of others lay dead or bleeding out. He didn't know which and didn't much care. Rather than waste time worrying about it, he simply grabbed the two guards who were facing away from him and smashed their heads together as hard as he could. Wounded or not, he was still strong. Their helmets shattered, and both of them fell flat and unmoving.

Not-Tina looked at him with a frown, assessing his damage. She didn't say anything, and neither did he. Sam merely pointed to the elevator door and Joe took the hint. The boy said something, but he couldn't hear the words. Not yet. He could feel a distinct itch that told him the damage he'd inflicted to himself was mending, but at a guess he would be at least another day or more before he could hear properly again.

His muscles shook with exhaustion, and Not-Tina—who was climbing behind him—had to help him stay on the ladder as they scaled their way to freedom.

When they were all at the top of the elevator shaft, Joe stared down into the hole at the bottom of the car. So much he'd planned to learn, and none of it had gone the way he'd wanted.

Evelyn would pay for that too. But later, after she'd had time to recover from the murder of her precious "son." For now, he was perfectly glad knowing that she was suffering.

Not-Tina pointed to a car as they left the building. The land-yacht was large and expensive and that suited him fine. She fished in her jeans pocket and pulled out car keys. He didn't want to ask, and even if he had, he couldn't have heard her answer.

Joe made it to the backseat before he collapsed. He was starving and exhausted and in pain and before he could think about anything else, he was also unconscious. Blood loss can do that to a person.

Chapter Fifty-Five

Sam Hall

SAM SUGGESTED THEY LEAVE the car a few miles from the hotel, and as much as all of them would have preferred to ride in luxury, they decided he was being smart. They left the keys in the ignition and the doors unlocked at a Wal-Mart parking lot, and then they walked the rest of the way. Since it was his suggestion, Sam got to carry Joe.

Hank was still exhausted and weak, but Not-Kyrie helped him get to the rooms.

They couldn't find the room keys, but Theresa put down the briefcase she'd stolen from the car long enough to pick the locks. Apparently Tina not only knew how to pick locks, she was also pretty mean at hot wiring cars, a fact that Theresa shared without hesitation.

No one bothered to point out that they would have been perfectly fine with getting to the hotel in another stolen car.

They were all too tired for the argument, and all very aware that a fight would have been inevitable if they'd chastised her. Besides, she'd come for them when she could have run off, and that meant more than walking a couple of miles.

There was no partying that night. While the Hydes usually liked a good celebration, they were all too sore and too tired. Instead Not-Kyrie walked to the closest convenience store and brought back bags of candy and junk food, and they ate in silence before they passed out.

All except for Joe, who did not wake up that night—not even when Theresa was cleaning his wounds and bandaging them as best she could using hotel towels and strips of the gray jumpsuits that most of them had been wearing.

Chapter Fifty-Six

Hunter Harrison

IN THE NIGHT THEY reverted, becoming smaller, weaker and arguably more human. All except Hank, who did not change, but slept as heavily as any of the others.

Not-Kyrie had been wise enough to put out the Do Not Disturb signs on the doors. They were not disturbed, and all of them slept the next day away, recovering from the stress and the chemicals that had left them sluggish and weakened.

When the next morning came, however, they awoke to the smell of fresh food and a great deal of coffee. Hank had gone out and grabbed a very large breakfast for the entire lot of them.

And if they all looked at Hank a little strangely, it was only because he was the only Other present as they ate and sorted through what had happened to all of them.

It was rough. As a unit they had slept through the entire

situation—except Hank, who had been in and out of a fever high enough to mess with his perceptions.

"So did we learn anything?" Hunter spoke after listening to the others try to piece everything together.

Tina looked at him and pointed to the briefcase. "Found the key for that in my pocket. I looked at the papers, but they don't mean much to me." She shrugged and looked at her feet. "I was never that good in school."

Gene looked at the contents of the briefcase while they ate, and he was the one who made the connections.

"This all belongs to someone named Josh Warburton. I think that's the name on your note to Evelyn Hunter? Anyway, a lot of this is just notes on expense accounts and the like, but there's a list of names here that I think is all of the kids who were adopted out like us. It's not complete—they don't all have current addresses—but there's a lot of names."

"What makes you sure they're all adopted out like us?" Kyrie leaned toward him and stared into his eyes with an intensity that made him look away and blush a bit.

"Simple. We're all on the list."

"We have to call them. We have to warn them." That was Kyrie again. She looked from one to the next of the group, practically willing them to agree with her.

Gene frowned at her. "With all due respect, why? Who are they to us?"

"They're like us, Gene. They need to be warned because no one deserves to get captured and locked away or worse." She looked toward Hank for a moment, then at Hunter, and it seemed she was almost afraid to finish her words. "We need to warn them, because they might not know what's waiting inside of them."

Hank shook his head. "That means Janus is going to figure out who we are soon enough. We can't call home again. Not unless we want these guys coming after our families." He grew silent for a moment.

"What's wrong?" Hunter saw the worry on the Other's face.

"I don't think Cody could go home either way."

"Why not?"

Hank held out his hands and shrugged. "Cody's in here, with me. We can talk to each other. But we can't change. I haven't been able to become Cody. I think maybe I'm stuck this way."

Kyrie quickly looked away. All of them understood what she was thinking and worrying about. If it could happen to Cody, it could happen to any of them. Suddenly, changing was looking like a dangerous proposition.

Hunter stood up and peered out the window of the hotel room, his skin crawling with the sensation that someone was watching him. It was almost a sure sign that Joe was waking up and wanted to get out.

Not yet, he prayed. *Not yet and not today.*

He was scared, though he wasn't quite sure why. He was also heartbroken. He'd seen his family—had spoken to his mother and his brother—and he ached to be with them again.

But he was scared, too. Because he had the damnedest feeling that something had gone wrong, and no idea where the notion was coming from.

But he would have bet a hundred dollars that Joe knew.

Chapter Fifty-Seven

Hank

YOU IN THERE?

Yeah. Cody's voice came back smooth and easy, like maybe they were standing right next to each other.

How are we going to do this? Are you going to try to make your folks understand?

Seriously, dude? I don't even understand it myself.

We let the body decide. It decided this was the best way for us to live, I guess. He paused for a moment and then asked, *You okay with this, Cody?*

I kind of have to be, don't I? Cody answered.

Well, yeah, I guess so.

Tell you one thing, though.

Yeah? What's that?

Hank could imagine the smile on Cody's face when he answered. *We ever get back to Ohio, I'm gonna beat the crap out of Wagner and Chadbourne myself.*

Hank chuckled. *Gotta say, it wasn't the least fun I've ever had. They've kind of losers.*

So let's get serious for a second. Can you actually hear their thoughts? The Others like you?

I have to work at it, but yeah. I can hear them. Sort of. I won't, though. It ain't cool. That's what started the fight between me and Joe. He just does whatever he wants, and that ain't cool at all.

So, can you influence their minds?

Hank took a while before he answered. *Maybe, why?*

I'll give you a dollar if you make Tina not yell at me anymore.

Hank laughed inside his head, and Cody joined him.

See, I thought you were going to ask me to make Kyrie fall for you.

You could do that? The absolute awe in Cody's voice was as hammed up as a can of Spam.

You wish, bro.

Yessiree, as a matter of fact I do. How are we going to get through this, Hank? What the heck are we? What did we become?

Hank shrugged. *Stronger, I think. I mean, look at Joe and Hunter. I bet they can't talk like this. I bet they can't work together like you and me can now. If they could, maybe they wouldn't be so worried about trying to stop each other.*

You think it could happen to the rest of them? What happened to us?

We didn't do it on purpose. We just figured out how to survive, Cody. If I knew how to make it happen for the others, I'd show them. But I don't know if Joe and Hunter could ever agree long enough to survive.

There was nothing to see, and yet he sense that Cody was nodding in agreement. They were both silent for a few moments and then Cody spoke again. *Shame about you not being able to control Kyrie, though. Be cool if you could make her like us.*

She already likes you.

Garbage. Cody laughed.

No, seriously, I saw the way she looked at you.

Dude, we share eyes, remember? Besides, she's a cheerleader. Digs guys with actual muscle tone, right?

Not sure if you noticed, bud, but we're kind of cut.

Cody chuckled in his head. *I guess we are. This new body thing is going to take getting used to. How are we going to do this? I mean, are you gonna be in charge all the time? Or are we going to take turns?*

We'll have to try to work out a schedule, I guess.

And what are we going to do about Joe?

Hank frowned. *Joe?*

Yeah. He kind of hates you, dude.

Guess we'll just have to watch our back until we figure all of this out.

Cody had no answer to that.

Chapter Fifty-Eight

Evelyn Hope

EVELYN AND GEORGE ATTENDED the funeral along with everyone else at the Boston compound. Gabriel had been well liked by his peers and admired by the adults who knew him.

And he had been loved by some too.

Evelyn allowed herself the luxury of tears, swearing it would only be the once in public. George cried with her. He had never known Gabriel very well, of course, but he cried for Evelyn. He understood her loss—her sorrow—and so he cried for her.

She promised herself she wouldn't hold that against him later. It didn't do to let people know of her weaknesses, not even someone she trusted as well as she trusted George.

The casket they lowered into the ground was empty, of course. Gabriel's body was taken for study, and it was best not to leave any evidence that could come back to haunt them later, anyway. When the studies were done, his body would be cremated. Still, she cried as the casket was lowered into the ground. And when George was tossing a handful of dirt onto the empty wooden box, Evelyn tugged at the gold chain around her neck until the fine metal links snapped and freed her wedding ring and the bronzed tooth from her Bobby.

She tossed her prized possession into the grave and watched without expression as the undertakers began burying the last of her family in the ground.

The time for sentiment was over.

Gabby was dead. Bobby was dead to her also. Even if she could separate him from Subject Seven, she would never be able to forgive his latest sin.

The attendees cried, of course. They had lost one of their own, a classmate and a good friend. She wasn't sure what they would do with the Strike Team now: they had never lost an Alpha before, excluding only Subject Seven. And as far as she knew, the Alphas had to come from the same group in order for a connection to exist. Still, that was a problem for another day.

There were more pressing matters to take care of.

She waited until the mourners had left and then waited until George calmed himself down.

"George?"

"Yes, Evelyn?"

"Did you double-check with Josh and his people regarding the tracking devices?"

"Yes, Evelyn. Of course. They were implanted in all of them, except the one with the snake tattoo."

"What was the effective range again?"

"No more than two miles, three on the outside." He spoke softly.

"Well, we'll have to work with what we have, won't we?"

"Yes, Evelyn."

"And George?"

"Yes, Evelyn?"

She looked around the cemetery, then down at the ground where her son should have been buried if he had been a real boy and not merely an experiment to which she had grown attached.

"Get the list of children adopted out from Josh and his people. And then have them killed."

George looked at her for several seconds, his mouth trembling. Finally he nodded. "Yes, Evelyn."

And that was why she kept him as her assistant. He was decidedly efficient and never questioned her when she was in the mood to be obeyed.

Chapter Fifty-Nine

Joe Bronx

HE HURT EVERYWHERE. NOT just physically—but in his mind, which was currently locked inside the darkness where it hid when Hunter was in charge.

Still, the pain was nothing new, not really. He'd been in constant pain for the first ten years of his life. Pain was an old friend, or at least an acquaintance who was feeling awfully familiar.

Gabby was dead. Evelyn was hurting. She was angry, and she was grieving and she probably wanted him dead and buried. And that meant they were finally on even footing.

For ten years he'd been forced to endure tortures and indignities, had been held captive and treated as nothing more than a lab rat. That would never happen again; he'd made himself a promise a long time ago, and though nothing had gone as he'd planned, he was still satisfied with the end results.

Evelyn was wounded. Even better, Hunter would be so very angry when he found out. And there was no way around the fact that Joe loved that thought. It soothed the aches in his mind and body alike to know that Hunter was going to absolutely lose his mind when he heard about this. And he would hear about it eventually. There was no way around that either. If he didn't read about it in a newspaper, he'd find out the next time one of Evelyn's new breed of soldiers encountered them.

Would there be a next time? Of course. He had no doubt about all of that. There would be a next time, because his mother would never forgive him now, and she was a relentless creature. He knew that from experience. She'd proven it to him a hundred times.

He tried to rise from the darkness, but Hunter pushed him back down. Fair enough. He could wait. He could be as patient as he needed to, because from now on Evelyn would bring the fight to him, and she would bring the fight to her precious "Bobby" as well.

If that was the best he could get from this encounter, it would have to be enough.